ADVERTISEMENT FOR DEATH

Wolfe picked up his current book from his desk, opened to his place, swiveled and maneuvered his seventh of a ton to a comfortable position and started reading. I went to my desk and sat, pulled the type-writer around, put in paper, and hit the keys. The first draft had some flaws, which I corrected. It was an ad for tomorrow's *Times*, reading like this:

"Woman with spider earrings and scratch on cheek who on Tuesday, driving a car, told boy at Thirty-fifth Street and Ninth Avenue to get a cop, please communicate with Nero Wolfe at address in phone book."

There wasn't one chance in a million it would get a nibble. But it did.

A NERO WOLFE MYSTERY

THE GOLDEN SPIDERS

REX STOUT

BANTAM BOOKS
TORONTO • NEW YORK • LONDON • SYDNEY

THE GOLDEN SPIDERS

*A Bantam Book / published by arrangement with
The Viking Press, Inc.*

PRINTING HISTORY
Viking edition published October 1953

Dollar Mystery edition published January 1954

Bantam edition / November 1955

2nd printing .. November 1955	6th printing ..... March 1969
3rd printnig ... January 1956	7th printing ..... March 1975
4th printing .... July 1964	8th printing .. November 1979
5th printing ..... March 1969	9th printing ...... April 1984

ISBN 0-553-23995-3

Published simultaneously in the United States and Canada

Bantam Books are published by Bantam Books, Inc. Its trademark, consisting of the words "Bantam Books" and the por-
trayal of a rooster, is Registered in U.S. Patent and Trademark
Office and in other countries. Marca Registrada. Bantam
Books, Inc., 666 Fifth Avenue, New York, New York 10103.

COVER PRINTED IN THE UNITED STATES OF AMERICA
TEXT PRINTED IN CANADA

U   18 17 16 15 14 13 12 11 10 9

THE
GOLDEN
SPIDERS

1 When the doorbell rings while Nero Wolfe and I are at dinner, in the old brownstone house on West Thirty-fifth Street, ordinarily it is left to Fritz to answer it. But that evening I went myself, knowing that Fritz was in no mood to handle a caller, no matter who it was.

Fritz's mood should be explained. Each year around the middle of May, by arrangement, a farmer who lives up near Brewster shoots eighteen or twenty starlings, puts them in a bag, and gets in his car and drives to New York. It is understood that they are to be delivered to our door within two hours after they were winged. Fritz dresses them and sprinkles them with salt, and, at the proper moment, brushes them with melted butter, wraps them in sage leaves, grills them, and arranges them on a platter of hot polenta, which is thick porridge of fine-ground yellow cornmeal with butter, grated cheese, and salt and pepper.

It is an expensive meal and a happy one, and Wolfe always looks forward to it, but that day he put on an exhibition. When the platter was brought in, steaming, and placed before him, he sniffed, ducked his head and sniffed again, and straightened to look up at Fritz.

"The sage?"

"No, sir."

"What do you mean, no, sir?"

"I thought you might like it once in a style I have suggested, with saffron and tarragon. Much fresh tarragon, with just a touch of saffron, which is the way—"

"Remove it!"

Fritz went rigid and his lips tightened.

"You did not consult me," Wolfe said coldly. "To find that without warning one of my favorite dishes has been radically altered is an unpleasant shock. It may possibly be edible, but I am in no humor to risk it. Please dispose of it and bring me four coddled eggs and a piece of toast."

1

Fritz, knowing Wolfe as well as I did, aware that this was a stroke of discipline that hurt Wolfe more than it did him and that it would be useless to try to parley, reached for the platter, but I put in, "I'll take some if you don't mind. If the smell won't keep you from enjoying your eggs?"

Wolfe glared at me.

That was how Fritz acquired the mood that made me think it advisable for me to answer the door. When the bell rang Wolfe had finished his eggs and was drinking coffee, really a pitiful sight, and I was toward the end of a second helping of the starlings and polenta, which was certainly edible. Going to the hall and the front, I didn't bother to snap the light switch because there was still enough twilight for me to see, through the one-way glass panel, that the customer on the stoop was not our ship coming in.

I pulled the door open and told him politely, "Wrong number."

I was polite by policy, my established policy of promoting the idea of peace on earth with the neighborhood kids. It made life smoother in that street, where there was a fair amount of ball throwing and other activities.

"Guess again," he told me in a low nervous alto, not too rude. "You're Archie Goodwin. I've gotta see Nero Wolfe."

"What's your name?"

"Pete."

"What's the rest of it?"

"Drossos. Pete Drossos."

"What do you want to see Mr. Wolfe about?"

"I gotta case. I'll tell him."

He was a wiry little specimen with black hair that needed a trim and sharp black eyes, the top of his head coming about level with the knot of my four-in-hand. I had seen him around the neighborhood but had nothing either for or against him. The thing was to ease him off without starting a feud, and ordinarily I would have gone at it, but after Wolfe's childish performance with Fritz I thought it would do him good to have another child to play with. Naturally he would snarl and snap, but if

Pete got scratched I could salve him afterward. So I invited him in and escorted him to the dining room.

Wolfe was refilling his coffee cup. He shot a glance at Pete, who I admit was not dressed up, put the pot down, looked straight at me, and spoke.

"Archie. I will not have interruptions at meals."

I nodded sympathetically. "I know, but this wasn't a meal. Call eggs a meal? This is Mr. Peter Drossos. He wants to consult you about a case. I was going to tell him you're busy, but I remembered you got sore because Fritz didn't consult you, and I didn't want you to get sore at Pete too. He's a neighbor of ours, and you know, love thy neighbor as thyself."

Ragging Wolfe is always a gamble. A quick reflex explosion may split the air; but if it doesn't, if he takes a second for a look at it, you're apt to find yourself topped. That time he took several seconds, sipping coffee, and then addressed our caller courteously. "Sit down, Mr. Drossos."

"I'm not mister, I'm Pete."

"Very well, Pete, sit down. Turn more to face me, please. Thank you. You wish to consult me?"

"Yeah, I gotta case."

"I always welcome a case, but the timing is a little unfortunate because Mr. Goodwin was going out this evening to see a billiard match, and now of course he will have to stay here to take down all that you say and all that I say. Archie, get your notebook, please?"

As I said, it's always a gamble. He had his thumb in my eye. I went across the hall to the office for a notebook and pen, and when I returned Fritz was there with coffee for me and cookies and a bottle of Coke for Pete. I said nothing. My pen and notebook would do the recording almost automatically, needing about a fifth of my brain, and I would see the rest of it devising plans for getting from under.

Pete was talking. "I guess it's okay him taking it down, but I gotta watch my end. This is strictly under the lid."

"If you mean it's confidential, certainly."

"Then I'll spill it. I know there's some private eyes you can't open up to, but you're different. We know all about you around here. I know how you feel about the lousy cops, just like I do. So I'll lay it out."

"Please do."

"Okay. What time is it?"

I looked at my wrist watch. "Ten to eight."

"Then it happened an hour ago. I know sometimes everything hangs on the time element, and right after it happened I went and looked at the clock in the drugstore near the corner, and it was a quarter to seven. I was working the wipe racket there at the corner of Thirty-fifth and Ninth, and a Caddy stopped—"

"Please. What's the wipe racket?"

"Why, you know, a car stops for the light and you hop to it with a rag and start wiping the window, and if it's a man and he lets you go on to the windshield you've got him for at least a dime. If it's a woman and she lets you go on, maybe you've got her and maybe not. That's a chance you take. Well, this Caddy stopped—"

"What's a Caddy?"

From the look that appeared in the sharp black eyes, Pete was beginning to suspect that he had picked the wrong private eye. I cut in to show him that anyhow one of us wasn't a moron, telling Wolfe, "A Cadillac automobile."

"I see. It stopped?"

"Yeah, for the light. I went for the window by the driver. It was a woman. She turned her face around to me to look straight at me and she said something. I don't think she made any sound, or anyway if she did I didn't hear anything through the window because it was up nearly to the top, but she worked her lips with it and I could tell what it was. She said, 'Help. Get a cop.' Like this, look."

He made the words with his lips, overdoing it some, without producing any noise. Wolfe nodded appreciatively. He turned to me. "Archie. Make a sketch of Pete's mouth doing that pantomime."

"Later," I said obligingly. "After you've gone to bed."

"It was plain as it could be," Pete went on. " 'Help, get a cop.' It hit me, it sure did. I tried to keep my face deadpan, I knew that was the way to take it, but I guess I didn't, because the man was looking at me and he—"

"Where was the man?"

"There on the seat with her. There was just them two in the car. I guess he saw by my face something had hit me, because he jabbed the gun against her harder and she jerked her head around—"

"Did you see the gun?"

"No, but I'm not a dope, am I? What else would make her want a cop and then jerk her head like that? What do you think it was, a lead pencil?"

"I prefer the gun. And then?"

"I backed up a little. All I had was a piece of rag, and him with a six gun. Now this next part—don't get me wrong, I got no use for cops. I feel about cops just like you. But it happened so quick I didn't realize just what I was doing, and I admit I looked around for a cop. I didn't see one, so I hopped to the sidewalk to see around the corner, and by the time I looked again the light had changed, and there went the car. I tried to flag another car to trail it, but nobody would stop. I thought I might catch it at Eighth Avenue and ran as fast as I could down Thirty-fifth, but it hit a green light at Eighth and went on through when I was only halfway there. But I got the license number."

He reached in his pants pocket, pulled out a little scrap of paper, and read from it: "Connecticut, Y,Y, nine, four, three, two."

"Excellent." Wolfe returned his empty cup to the saucer. "Have you given that to the police?"

"Me?" Pete was scornful. "The cops? Look, am I screwy? I go to the precinct and tell a flattie, or even say I get to a sarge and tell him, and what? First he don't believe me and then he chases me and then I'm marked. It don't hurt you to be marked, because you're a private eye with a license and you've got something on a lot of inspectors."

"I have? What?"

"Don't ask me. But everybody knows you're loaded with dirt on some big boys or you'd have been rubbed out long ago. But a kid like me can't risk it to be marked even if I'm straight. I hate cops, but you don't have to be a crook to hate cops. I keep telling my mother I'm straight, and I am straight, but I'm telling you it takes a lot of guts. What do you think of this case I got?"

Wolfe considered. "It seems a little—uh—hazy."

"Yeah, that's why I came to you. I went to a place I go to when I want to think, and I went all over it. I saw it was a swell case if I handled it right. The car was a Caddy, a dark gray fifty-two Caddy. The man looked mean, but he looked like dough, he looked like he might have two or three more Caddies. The woman did too. She wasn't as old as my mother, but I guess I can't go by that because my mother has done a lot of hard work, and I bet she never did work. She had a scratch on her face, on her left cheek, and her face was all twisted saying that to me, 'Help, get a cop'; but, thinking it over, I decided she was a good-looker. She had big gold spiders for earrings, spiders with their legs stretched out. Pure gold."

Wolfe grunted.

"Okay," Pete conceded, "they looked like gold. They wasn't brass. Anyhow, the whole layout said dough, and what I was thinking went like this: I got a case with people with dough, and how do I handle it so I'll get some? There might be up to fifty dollars in it if I handle it right. If he kills her I can identify him and get the reward. I can tell what she said to me and how he jabbed the gun in her—"

"You didn't see a gun."

"That's a detail. If he didn't kill her, if he just made her do something or tell him something or give him something, I can go and put it up to him, either he comes across with fifty bucks, or maybe a hundred, or I hang it on him."

"That would be blackmail."

"Okay." Pete brushed cooky crumbs from his fingers onto the tray. "That's why I decided I had to see you after I thought it over. I saw I couldn't handle it alone and I'd have to cut you in, but you understand it's my case. Maybe you think I was a sap to tell you that license number before we made a deal, but I don't. If you get onto him and corner him and try to cross me and hog it, I'll still have to identify him, so it will be up to me. If blackmail's out, you can figure it so it's not blackmail. What do you say we split fifty-fifty?"

"I'll tell you, Pete." Wolfe pushed his chair back and got his bulk comfortably settled in a new position. "If we are to join hands on your case I think I should tell you a few things about the science and art of detection. Mr.

Goodwin will of course take it down, and when he types it he will make a copy for you. But first he'll make a phone call. Archie, you have that license number. Call Mr. Cramer's office and give them that number. Say that you have information that that car, or its owner or operator, may have been involved in a violation of a law in this city in the past two hours, and suggest a routine check. Do not be more definite. Say that our information is unverified and inquiry should be discreet."

"Hey," Pete demanded, "who's Mr. Cramer? A cop?"

"A police inspector," Wolfe told him. "You yourself suggested the possibility of murder. If there was a murder there is a corpse. If there is a corpse it should be found. Unless and until it is found, where's your case? We have no idea where to look for it, so we'll trick the police into finding it for us. I often make use of them that way. Archie. Of course you will not mention Pete's name, since he doesn't want to be marked."

As I went across to the office, to my desk, and dialed the number of Manhattan Homicide West, I was reflecting that of all Wolfe's thousand techniques for making himself obnoxious the worst was when he thought he was being funny. When I finished talking to Sergeant Purley Stebbins and hung up, I was tempted to just walk out and go up to watch Mosconi and Watrous handle their cues, but of course that wouldn't do because it would have been admitting he had called me good, and he would merely have shooed Pete out and settled down with a book and a satisfied smirk.

So I marched back to the dining room, sat down and took up my pen, and said brightly, "All right, they're alerted. Shoot the lecture on detection, and don't leave anything out."

Wolfe leaned back, put his elbows on the chair arms, and matched his fingertips. "You understand, Pete, that I shall confine myself to the problems and methods of the private detective who works at his profession for a living."

"Yeah." Pete had a fresh bottle of Coke. "That's what I want, how to rake in the dough."

"I had remarked that tendency in you. But you must not permit it to smother other considerations. It is desirable that you should earn your fees, but it is essential that you feel you have earned them, and that depends partly on your ego. If your ego is healthy and hardy, as mine is, you will seldom have difficulty—"

"What's my ego?"

"There are various definitions, philosophical, metaphysical, psychological, and now psychoanalytical, but as I am using the term it means the ability to play up everything that raises your opinion of yourself and play down everything that lowers it. Is that clear?"

"I guess so." Pete was frowning in concentration. "You mean, do you like yourself or don't you."

"Not precisely, but that's close enough. With a robust ego, your feeling—"

"What's robust?"

Wolfe made a face. "I'll try to use words you have met before, but when I don't, when one of them is a stranger to you, kindly do not interrupt. If you are smart enough to be a good detective, you are smart enough to guess accurately the meaning of a new word by the context— which means the other words I use with it. Also there is usually a clue. A moment ago I spoke of a healthy and hardy ego, and then, after your interruption, I spoke of a robust ego in the same connection. So obviously 'robust' means 'healthy and hardy,' and if you have the stuff of a good detective in you, you should have spotted it. How old are you?"

"Twelve."

"Then I should make allowances, and do. To continue: with a robust ego, your feeling about earning your fees can safely be left to your intelligence and common sense. Never collect or accept a fee that you feel you haven't earned; if you do, your integrity crumbles and your ego will have worms. With that one reservation, get all you can. As you must not take what you feel you haven't earned, so must you get what you feel you have earned. Don't even discuss a case with a prospective client until you know about his ability to pay. So much—"

"Then why—" Pete blurted, and stopped.

"Why what?"

"Nothing. Only you're discussing with me, just a kid."

"This is a special case. Mr. Goodwin brought you in to

me, and he is my trusted and highly valuable assistant, and he would be disappointed if I didn't explore your affair thoroughly and let him take it down and type it." Wolfe favored me with a hypocritical glance and returned to Pete. "So much for your ego and your fees. As for your methods, they must of course be suited to your field. I pass over such fields as industrial espionage and divorce evidence and similar repugnant snooperies, since the ego of any man who engages in them is already infested with worms, and so you are not concerned. But take robbery. Say, for instance, a woman's jewel box has been looted, and she doesn't want to go to the police because she suspects—"

"Let's take murder. I'd rather start with murder."

"As you will." Wolfe was gracious. "You're getting this, are you, Archie?"

"You bet. With my tongue out."

"Good. But robbery or murder, no matter what, speaking generally, you must thoroughly understand that primarily you are practicing an art, not a science. The role of science in crime detection is worthy, honorable, and effective, but it has little part in the activities of a private detective who aspires to eminence. Anyone of moderate capacity can become adept with a vernier caliper, a camera, a microscope, a spectrograph, or a centrifuge, but they are merely the servants of detection. Science in detection can be distinguished, even brilliant, but it can never replace either the inexorable march of a fine intellect through a jungle of lies and fears to the clearing of truth, or the flash of perception along a sensitive nerve touched off by a tone of a voice or a flicker of an eye."

"Excuse me," I interposed. "Was that 'a tone of voice' or 'a tone of a voice'?"

"Neither," Wolfe lied. "It was 'a tone of some voice.'" He resumed to Pete, "The art of detection has many levels and many faces. Take one. Shadowing a man around New York without losing him is an extremely difficult task. When the police undertake it seriously they use three men, and even so they are often hoodwinked. There is a man who often works for me, Saul Panzer, who is a genius at it, working alone. I have discussed it with him and have concluded that he himself does not know the secret of his superlative knack. It is not a conscious and controlled operation of his brain, though he has a good one; it is something hidden somewhere in his nervous system—possibly, of course, in his skull. He says that he seems somehow to know, barely in the nick of time, what the man he is following is about to do—not what he has done or is doing, but what he intends. That's why Mr. Panzer might teach you everything he knows, and still you would never be his equal. But that doesn't mean you shouldn't learn all you can. Learning will never hurt you. Only the man who knows too little knows too much. It is only when you undertake to use what you have learned that you discover whether you can transform knowledge into performance."

Wolfe aimed a thumb at me. "Take Mr. Goodwin. It would be difficult for me to function effectively without him. He is irreplaceable. Yet his actions are largely governed by impulse and caprice, and that would of course incapacitate him for any important task if it were not that he has somewhere concealed in him—possibly in his brain, though I doubt it—a powerful and subtle governor. For instance, the sight of a pretty girl provokes in him an overwhelming reaction of appreciation and approval, and correlatively his acquisitive instinct, but he has never married. Why not? Because he knows that if he had a wife his reaction to pretty girls, now pure and frank and free, would not only be intolerably adulterated but would also be under surveillance and subject to restriction by authority. So the governor always stops him short of disaster, doubtless occasionally on the very brink. It works similarly with the majority of his impulses and whims, but now and then it fails to intervene in time, and he suffers mishap, as this evening when he was impelled to badger me when a certain opportunity offered. It has already cost him—what time is it, Archie?"

I looked. "Eighteen minutes to nine."

"Hey!" Pete leaped from his chair. "I gotta run! My mother—I gotta be home by a quarter to! See you tomorrow!"

He was on his way. By the time I was up and in the hall he had reached the front door and pulled it open, and was gone. I stepped to the threshold of the dining room and told Wolfe, "Damn it, I was hoping he would stay till midnight so you could finish. After that a billiard match will be pretty dull, but I might as well go."

I went.

2 Next day, Wednesday, I was fairly busy. A hardware manufacturer from Youngstown, Ohio, had come to New York to try to locate a son who had cut his lines of communication, and had wired Wolfe to help, and we had Saul Panzer, Fred Durkin, and Orrie Cather out scouting around. That kept me close to my desk and the phone, getting reports and relaying instructions.

A little after four in the afternoon Pete Drossos showed up and wanted to see Wolfe. His attitude indicated that while he was aware that I too had a license as a private detective and he had nothing serious against me, he preferred to deal with the boss. I explained that Nero Wolfe spent four hours every day—from nine to eleven in the morning and from four to six in the afternoon—up in the plant rooms on the roof, with his ten thousand orchids, bossing Theodore Horstmann instead of me, and that during those hours he was unavailable. Pete let me know that he thought that was a hell of a way for a private eye to spend his time, and I didn't argue the point. By the time I finally got him eased out to the stoop and the door closed, I was ready to concede that maybe my governor needed oiling. Pete was going to be a damn nuisance, no doubt of it. I should have choked my impulse to invite him in as a playmate for Wolfe. Whenever I catch myself talking me into chalking one up against me, it helps to take a drink, so I went to the kitchen for a glass of milk. As I returned to the office the phone was ringing—Orrie Cather making a report.

At the dinner table that evening neither Wolfe nor Fritz gave the slightest indication that starlings had ever come between them. As Wolfe took his second helping of the main dish, which was Danish pork pancake, he said distinctly, "Most satisfactory." Since for him that was positively lavish, Fritz took it as offered, nodded with dignity, and murmured, "Certainly, sir." So there were no sparks flying when we finished our coffee, and Wolfe was so agreeable that he said he would like to see me demonstrate Mosconi's spectacular break shot I had told him about, if I cared to descend to the basement with him.

But I didn't get to demonstrate. When the doorbell rang as we were leaving the dining room, I supposed of course it was Pete, but it wasn't. The figure visible through the glass panel was fully twice as big as Pete, and much more familiar—Sergeant Purley Stebbins of Manhattan Homicide West. Wolfe went into the office, and I went to the front and opened the door.

"They went thataway," I said, pointing.

"Nuts. I want to see Wolfe. And you."

"This is me. Shoot."

"And Wolfe."

"He's digesting pork. Hold it." I slipped the chain bolt to hold the door to a two-inch crack, stepped to the office, told Wolfe Stebbins wanted an audience, stood patiently while he made faces, was instructed to bring the caller in, and returned to the front and did so.

Over the years a routine had been established for seating Sergeant Stebbins in our office. When he came with Inspector Cramer, Cramer of course took the big red leather chair near the end of Wolfe's desk, and Purley one of the yellow ones, which were smaller. When he came alone, I tried to herd him into the red leather chair but never made it. He always sidestepped and pulled up a yellow one. It wasn't that he felt a sergeant shouldn't sit where he had seen an inspector sit, not Purley. It may be he doesn't like to face a window, or possibly he just doesn't like red chairs. Some day I'll ask him.

That day he got his meat and muscle, of which he has a full share, at rest on a yellow chair as usual, eyed Wolfe a moment, and then twisted his neck to confront me. "Yesterday you phoned me about a car—a dark gray fifty-two Cadillac, Connecticut license YY nine-four-three-two. Why?"

I raised my shoulders and let them drop. "I told you.

We had information, not checked, that the car or its owner or driver might have been involved in something, or might be. I suggested a routine inquiry."

"I know you did. Exactly what was your information and where did you get it?"

I shook my head. "You asked me that yesterday and I passed it. I still pass. Our informant doesn't want to be annoyed."

"Well, he's going to be. Who was it and what did he tell you?"

"Nothing doing." I turned a hand over. "You know damn well this is just a bad habit you've got. If something has happened that makes you think I've got to tell you who and what, tell me what happened and let's see if I agree with you. You know how reasonable I am."

"Yeah, I sure do." Purley set his jaw and then relaxed it. "At six-forty this afternoon, two hours ago, a car stopped for a red light at the corner of Thirty-fifth Street and Ninth Avenue. A boy with a rag went to it and started wiping a window. He finished that side and started for the other side, and as he was circling in front of the car it suddenly jumped forward and ran over him, and kept going fast, across the avenue and along Thirty-fifth Street. The boy died soon after the ambulance got him to the hospital. The driver was a man, alone in the car. With excitement like that people never see much, but two people, a woman and a boy, agree about the license number, Connecticut YY nine-four-three-two, and the boy says it was a dark gray Cadillac sedan. Well?"

"What was the boy's name? The one that was killed."

"What's that got to do with it?"

"I don't know. I'm asking."

"His name was Drossos. Peter Drossos."

I swallowed. "That's just fine. The sonofabitch."

"Who, the boy?"

"No." I turned to Wolfe. "Do you tell it or do I?"

Wolfe had closed his eyes. He opened them to say, "You," and closed them again.

I didn't think it was necessary to tell Stebbins about the domestic crisis that had given me the impulse to take Pete in to Wolfe, but I gave him everything that was relevant, including Pete's second visit that afternoon. Though for once in his life he was satisfied that he was getting something straight in that office, he asked a lot of questions, and at the end he saw fit to contribute an unfriendly comment to the effect that worthy citizens like Nero Wolfe and Archie Goodwin might have been expected to show a little more interest in a woman with a gun in her ribs wanting a cop.

I wasn't feeling jaunty, and that stung me. "Specimens like you," I told him, "are not what has made this country great. The kid might have made it all up. He admitted he didn't see the gun. Or the woman might have been pulling his leg. If I had told you yesterday who had told me what, you would have thought I was screwy to spend a dime on it for a phone call. And I did give you the license number. Did you check on it?"

"Yes. It was a floater. It was taken from a Plymouth that was stolen in Hartford two months ago."

"No trace?"

"None so far. Now we'll ask Connecticut to dig. I don't know how many floater plates there are in New York this minute, but there are plenty."

"How good a description have you got of the driver?"

"We've got four and no two alike. Three of them aren't worth a damn and the other one may be—a man that had just come out of the drugstore and happened to notice the kid going to the car with his rag. He says the driver was a man about forty, dark brown suit, light complexion, regular features, felt hat pulled down nearly to his ears. He says he thinks he could identify him." Purley got up. "I'll be going. I'll admit I'm disappointed. I fully expected either I'd get a lead from you or I'd find you covering for a client."

Wolfe opened his eyes. "I wish you luck, Mr. Stebbins. That boy ate at my table yesterday."

"Yeah," Purley growled, "that makes it bad. People have no business running over boys that ate at your table."

On that sociable note he marched out, and I went to the hall with him. As I put my hand on the doorknob a figure rose to view outside, coming up the steps to the stoop, and when I pulled the door open there she was—a skinny little woman in a neat dark blue dress, no jacket and no hat, with puffed red eyes and her mouth pressed so tight there were no lips.

Stebbins was just back of me as I addressed her. "Can I help you, madam?"

She squeezed words out. "Does Mr. Nero Wolfe live here?"

I told her yes.

"Do you think I could see him? I won't be long. My name is Mrs. Anthea Drossos."

She had been crying and looked as if she might resume any second, and a crying woman is one of the things Wolfe won't even try to take. So I told her he was busy, and I was his confidential assistant, and wouldn't she please tell me.

She raised her head to meet my eyes straight. "My boy Pete told me to see Mr. Nero Wolfe," she said, "and I'll just wait here till I can see him." She propped herself against the railing of the stoop.

I backed up and shut the door. Stebbins was at my heels as I entered the office and spoke to Wolfe. "Mrs. Anthea Drossos wants to see you. She says her boy Pete told her to. I won't do. She'll camp on the stoop all night if she has to. She might start crying in your presence. What do I do, take a mattress out to her?"

That opened his eyes all right. "Confound it. What can I do for the woman?"

"Nothing. Me too. But she won't take it from me."

"Then why the devil—pfui! Bring her in. That performance of yours yesterday—bring her in."

I went and got her. When I ushered her in Purley was planted back in his chair. With my hand on her elbow because she didn't seem any too sure of her footing, I steered her to the red leather number, which would have held three of her. She perched on the edge, with her black eyes—blacker, I suppose, because of the contrast with the inflamed lids—aimed at Wolfe.

Her voice was low and a little quavery, but determined. "Are you Mr. Nero Wolfe?"

He admitted it. She shifted the eyes to me, then to Stebbins, and back to Wolfe. "These gentlemen?" she asked.

"Mr. Goodwin, my assistant, and Mr. Stebbins, a policeman who is invesigating the death of your son."

She nodded. "I thought he looked like a cop. My boy Pete wouldn't want me to tell this to a cop."

From her tone and expression it seemed pretty plain that she didn't intend to do anything her boy Pete wouldn't have wanted her to do, and therefore we had a problem. With Purley's deep suspicion that Wolfe, not to mention me, would rather be caught dead than with nothing up his sleeve, he sure wasn't going to bow out. But without hesitation he arose, said, "I'll go to the kitchen," and headed for the door. My surprise lasted half a second, until I realized where he was going. In the alcove at the rear end of the hall, across from the kitchen, there was a hole in the wall that partitioned the alcove from the office. On the office side the hole was covered with a trick picture, and from the alcove side, when you slid a panel, you could see and hear movements and sounds from the office. Purley knew all about it.

As Purley disappeared I thought it just as well to warn Wolfe. "The picture."

"Certainly," Wolfe said peevishly. He looked at Mrs. Drossos. "Well, madam?"

She was taking nothing for granted. She got up and went to the open door to look both ways in the hall, shut the door, and returned to her seat. "You know Pete got killed."

"Yes, I know."

"They told me, and I ran down to the street, and there he was. He was unconscious but he wasn't dead. They let me ride in the ambulance with him. That was when he told me. He opened—"

She stopped. I was afraid it was going to bust, and so was she, but after sitting for half a minute without a muscle moving she had it licked and could go on. "He opened his eyes and saw me, and I put my head down to him. He said —I think I can tell you just what he said—he said, 'Tell Nero Wolfe he got me. Don't tell anybody but Nero Wolfe. Give him my money in the can.'"

She stopped and was rigid again. After a full minute of it Wolfe nudged her. "Yes, madam?"

She opened her bag, of black leather that had seen some wear but was good for more, fingered in it, extracted a small package wrapped in paper, and arose to put the package on Wolfe's desk.

"There's four dollars and thirty cents." She stayed on her feet. "He made it himself, it's his money that he kept in a tobacco can. That was the last thing he said, telling me to give you his money in the can; after that he was unconscious again, and he died before they could do anything at the hospital. I came away and came home to get his money and come and tell you. Now I'll go back." She turned, took a couple of steps, and turned again. "Did you understand what I told you?"

"Yes, I understand."

"Do you want me to do anything?"

"No, I think not. Archie?"

I was already there beside her. She seemed a little steadier on her feet than she had coming in, but I kept her arm anyway, on out to the stoop and down the seven steps to the sidewalk. She didn't thank me, but since she may not even have known I was there I didn't hold it against her.

Purley was in the hall when I re-entered, with his hat on. I asked him, "Did you shut the panel?"

"Taking candy from a kid I might expect," he said offensively. "But taking candy from a dead kid, by God!"

He was leaving, and I sidestepped to block him. "Oaf. Meaning you. If we had insisted on her taking it back she would have—"

I chopped it off at his grin of triumph. "Got you that time!" he croaked, and brushed past me and went.

So as I stepped into the office I was biting a nail. It is not often that Purley Stebbins can string me, but that day he had caught me off balance because my sentiments had been involved. Naturally I reacted by trying to take it out on Wolfe. I went to his desk for the little packet, unfolded the paper, and arranged the contents neatly in front of him: two dollar bills, four quarters, nine dimes, and eight nickels.

"Right," I announced. "Four dollars and thirty cents. Hearty congratulations. After income tax and deducting ten cents for expenses—the phone call to Stebbins yesterday—there will be enough left to—"

"Shut up," he snapped. "Will you return it to her tomorrow?"

"I will not. Nor any other day. You know damn well that's impossible."

"Give it to the Red Cross."

"You give it." I was firm. "She may never come again, but if she does and asks me what we did with Pete's money I won't feel like saying Red Cross and I won't feel like lying."

He pushed the dough away from him, to the other edge of the desk, toward me. "You brought him into this house."

"It's your house, and you fed him cookies."

That left it hanging. Wolfe picked up his current book from the other end of his desk, opened to his place, swiveled and maneuvered his seventh of a ton to a comfortable position, and started reading. I went to my desk and sat, and pretened to go over yesterday's reports from Saul and Fred and Orrie while I considered the situation. Somewhat later I pulled the typewriter around, put in paper, and hit the keys. The first draft had some flaws, which I corrected, and then typed it again on a fresh sheet. That time I thought it would do. I turned to face Wolfe and announced, "I have a suggestion."

He finished his paragraph, which must have been a long one, before glancing at me. "Well?"

"We're stuck with this dough and have to do something with it. You may remember that you told Pete that the point is not so much to earn a fee as it is to feel that you earned it. I should think you would feel you earned this one if you blow it all on an ad in the paper reading something like this:

"Woman with spider earrings and scratch on cheek who on Tuesday, driving a car, told boy at Thirty-fifth Street and Ninth Avenue to get a cop, please communicate with Nero Wolfe at address in phone book."

I slid the paper across his desk to him. "In the *Times* the fee might not quite cover it, but I'll be glad to toss in a buck or two. I regard it as brilliant. It will spend Pete's money on Pete. It will make Cramer and Stebbins sore, and Stebbins has it coming to him. And since there's not one chance in a million that it will get a nibble, it won't expose you to the risk of any work or involvement. Last but not least, it will get your name in the paper. What do you say?"

He picked up the sheet and glanced over it with his nose turned up. "Very well," he agreed grumpily. "I hope to heaven this has taught you a lesson."

3 The hardware manufacturer's son was finally spotted and corralled the next day, Thursday afternoon. Since that was a hush operation for more reasons than one—to show you how hush, he wasn't a hardware manufacturer and he wasn't from Youngstown—I can supply no details. But I make one remark. If Wolfe felt that he earned the fee he soaked that bird for, no ego was ever put to a severer test.

So Thursday was a little hectic, with no spare time for consideration of the question whether, if we had taken a different slant on the case Pete had come to share with us, Pete might still be breathing. In the detective business there are plenty of occasions for that kind of consideration, and while there is no percentage in letting it get you down, it doesn't hurt to take time out now and then for some auditing.

It had been too late Wednesday night to get the ad in for Thursday. Friday morning I had to grin at myself a couple of times. When I went down the two flights from my bedroom and entered the kitchen, the first thing I did after greeting Fritz was to turn to the ads in the Times for a look at ours. That rated a grin. It meant nothing, either professionally or personally, since the chance of getting an answer was even slimmer than my estimate of one in a million. The second grin came later, when I was dealing with corn muffins and sausage—Fritz having taken Wolfe's breakfast tray up to him according to schedule—with the Times in front of me on the rack, and the phone rang and I nearly knocked my chair over getting up to go for it. It was not someone answering the ad. Some guy on Long Island wanted to know if we could let him have three plants in bloom of Vanda caerulea. I told him we didn't sell plants, and anyway that Vandas didn't bloom in May.

But Pete's case was brought to us again before noon, though not by way of the ad. Wolfe had just got down to the office from the plant rooms and settled himself at his desk for a look at the morning mail when the doorbell rang. Going to the hall and seeing the ringer through the one-way panel, I had no need to proceed to the door to ask him what he wanted. That customer always wanted to see Wolfe, and his arriving on the dot of eleven made it certain.

I turned and told Wolfe, "Inspector Cramer."

He scowled at me. "What does he want?" Childish again.

"Shall I ask him?"

"Yes. No. Very well."

I went and let him in. From the way he grunted a greeting, if it could be called a greeting, and from the expression on his face, he had not come to give Wolfe a medal. Cramer's big red face and burly figure never inspire a feeling of good-fellowship, but he had his ups and downs, and that morning he was not up. He preceded me to the office, gave Wolfe the twin of the greeting he had given me, lowered himself into the red leather chair, and aimed a cold stare at Wolfe. Wolfe returned it.

"Why did you put that ad in the paper?" Cramer demanded.

Wolfe turned away from him and fingered in the little stack of papers on his desk that had just been removed from envelopes. "Archie," he said, "this letter from Jordan is farcical. He knows quite well that I do not use Brassavolas in tri-generic crosses. He doesn't deserve an answer, but he'll get one. Your notebook. 'Dear Mr. Jordan. I am aware that you have had ill success with—'"

"Save it," Cramer rasped. "Okay. Putting an ad in the paper is not a felony, but I asked a civil question."

"No," Wolfe said with finality. "Civil?"

"Then put it your way. You know what I want to know. How do you want me to ask it?"

"I would first have to be told why you want to know."

"Because I think you're covering something or somebody that's connected with a homicide. Which has been known to happen. From what you told Stebbins yesterday, you have no interest in the killing of that boy, and you have no client. Then you wouldn't spend a bent nickel on it, not you, and you certainly wouldn't start an inquiry that might make you use up energy. I might have asked you flat, who's your client, but no, I stick to the simple fact why did you run that ad. If that's not civil, civilize it and then tell me."

Wolfe took in a long-drawn sigh and let it out. "Archie. Tell him, please."

I obliged. It didn't take long, since he already had Purley's report, and I had merely to explain how we had decided to disburse Pete's money, to which I had added $1.85 of my own. Meanwhile Cramer's hard gray eyes were leveled at me. I had often had to meet those eyes and stall or cover or dodge, so they didn't bother me any when I was merely handing it over straight.

When he had asked a couple of questions and had been answered, he moved the eyes to Wolfe and inquired abruptly, "Have you ever seen or heard of a man named Matthew Birch?"

"Yes," Wolfe said shortly.

"Oh. You have." A gleam showed in the gray eyes for a fraction of a second. If I hadn't known them so well I wouldn't have caught it. "I intend to make this civil. Would you mind telling me when and where?"

"No. In the *Gazette* day before yesterday, Wednesday. As you know, I never leave this house on business, and leave it as seldom as may be for anything whatever, and I depend on newspapers and the radio to keep me informed of the concerns and activities of my fellow beings. As reported, the body of a man named Matthew Birch was found late Tuesday night—or Wednesday, rather, around three a.m.—in a cobbled alley alongside a South Street pier. It was thought that a car had run over him."

"Yeah. I'll try to frame this right. Except for newspaper or radio items connected with his death, had or have you ever seen or heard of him?"

"Not under that name."

"Damn it, under any name?"

"Not to my knowledge."

"Have you any reason to suppose or suspect that the man found dead in that alley was someone you had ever seen or heard of in any connection whatever?"

"That's more like it," Wolfe said approvingly. "That should settle it. The answer is no. May I ask one? Have you any reason to suppose or suspect that the answer should be yes?"

Cramer didn't reply. He tilted his head until his chin touched the knot of his tie, pursed his lips, regarded me for a long moment, and then went back to Wolfe. He spoke. "This is why I came. With the message the boy sent you by his mother, and the way the car jumped him from a standstill and then tore off, already it didn't look like any accident, and now there are complications, and when I find complicated trouble and you even remotely involved I want to know exactly where and how you got on—and where you get off."

"I asked about reasons, not about animus."

"There's no animus. Here's the complication. The car that killed the boy was found yesterday morning, with that floater Connecticut plate still on it, parked up on One Hundred and Eighty-sixth Street. Laboratory men worked on it all day. They cinched it that it killed the boy, but not only that, underneath it, caught tight where an axle joins a rod, they found a piece of cloth the size of a man's hand. That piece of cloth was the flap torn from the jacket which was on the body of Matthew Birch when it was found. The laboratory is looking for further evidence that it was that car that killed Birch, but I'm no hog and I don't need it. Do you?"

Wolfe was patient. "For a working hypothesis, if I were working on it, no."

"That's the point. You are working on it. You put that ad in."

Wolfe's head wagged slowly from side to side to punctuate his civilized forbearance. "I'll stipulate," he conceded, "that I am capable of flummery, that I have on occasion gulled and hoaxed you, but you know I eschew the crudeness of an explicit lie. I tell you that the facts we have given you in this matter are guileless and complete, that I have no client connected with it in any way, and that I am not engaged in it and do not intend to be. I certainly agree—"

The phone ringing stopped him. I got it at my desk. "Nero Wolfe's office, Archie Goodwin speaking."

"May I speak to Mr. Wolfe, please?" The voice was low, nervous, and feminine.

"I'll see if he's available. Your name?"

"He wouldn't know my name. I want to see him—it's about his advertisement in the *Times* this morning. I want to make an appointment with him."

I kept it casual. "I handle his appointments. May I have your name, please?"

"I'd rather—when I come. Could I come at twelve o'clock?"

"Hold the wire a minute." I consulted my desk calendar, turning to a page for next week. "Yes, that'll be all right if you're punctual. You have the address?"

She said she did. I hung up and turned to report to Wolfe. "A character who probably wants to look at the orchids. I'll handle it as usual."

He resumed to Cramer. "I certainly agree that the evidence that the boy and Matthew Birch were killed by the same car is a noteworthy complication, but actually that should make it simpler for you. Even though the license plate is useless, surely you can trace the car itself."

Cramer's expression had reverted to the cold stare he had started with. "I have never had any notion," he stated, "that you are a crude liar. I have never seen you crude." He arose. In Wolfe's presence he always made a point of getting upright from a chair with the leverage of his leg muscles only, because Wolfe used hands and arms. "No," he said, "not crude," and turned and marched out.

I went to the hall to see the door close behind him and then returned to the office and my desk.

"The letter to Mr. Jordan," Wolfe instructed me.

"Yes, sir." I got my notebook. "First, though, I still say it was one in a million, but the one turned up this time. That was a woman on the phone about the ad. No name, and I didn't want to press her with company present. She made an appointment for noon today."

"With whom?"

"You."

His lips tightened. He released them. "Archie. This is insufferable."

"I know damn well it is. But considering that Cramer wasn't being civilized, I thought it might be satisfactory to have a little chat with her before phoning him to come and get her." I glanced up at the wall clock. "She'll be here in twenty minutes—if she comes."

He grunted. " 'Dear Mr. Jordan . . .' "

4

She came. She was much more ornamental in the red leather chair than Inspector Cramer, or, for that matter, most of the thousands of tenants I had seen in it, but she sure was nervous. At the door, after I opened it and invited her in, I thought she was going to turn and scoot, and so did she, but she finally made her legs take her over the sill and let me conduct her to the office.

The scratch on her left cheek, on a slant down toward the corner of her mouth, was faint but noticeable on her smooth fair skin, and it was no wonder that Pete, looking straight at her face, had taken in the spider earrings. I agreed with him that they were gold, and they were fully as noticeable as the scratch. In spite of the scratch and the earrings and the jerky nervousness, on her the red leather chair looked good. She was about my age, which was not ideal, but I have nothing against maturity if it isn't overdone.

When Wolfe asked her, not too grumpily, what he could do for her, she opened her bag and got out two pieces of paper. The bag was of soft green suede, the same as the jacket she wore over a dark green woolen dress, and also the cocky little pancake tilted to one side of her head. It was an ensemble if I ever saw one.

"This," she said, "is just a clipping of your advertisement." She returned it to the bag. "This is a check made out to you for five hundred dollars."

"May I see it, please?"

"I don't—not yet. It has my name on it."

"So I would guess."

"I want to ask you—some things before I give you my name."

"What things?"

"Well, I—about the boy. The boy I asked to get a cop."
Her voice wouldn't have been bad at all, in fact I might
have liked it, if it hadn't been so jumpy. She was getting
more nervous instead of less. "I want to see him. Will
you arrange for me to see him? Or it would be—just give
me his name and address. I think perhaps that would be
enough for the five hundred dollars—I know you charge
high. Or I might want—but first tell me that."

Wolfe invariably kept his eyes, when they were open,
directly at the person he was talking to, but it had struck
me that he was giving this visitor a specially keen inspec-
tion. He turned to me. "Archie. Please look closely at the
scratch on her cheek."

I got up to obey. She had alternatives: sit and let me
look, cover her face with her hands, or get up and go; but
before she had time to choose I was there, bending over,
with my eyes only a foot from her face.

She started to say something, then checked it as I
straightened up and told Wolfe, "Made with something
with a fine sharp point. It could have been a needle, but
more likely a small scissors point."

"When?"

"The best guess is today, but it could have been yesterday I suppose. Not possibly three days ago." I stayed beside
her.

"This is impudent!" she blurted. She left the chair.
"I'm glad I didn't tell you my name!" She couldn't sweep
out without sweeping through me.

"Nonsense." Wolfe was curt. "You couldn't possibly
have imposed on me, even without the evidence of the
scratch, unless you had been superlatively coached. Describe the boy. Describe the other occupants of the car.
What time did it happen? What did the boy say? Exactly
what did he do? And so on. As for your name, that is no
longer in your discretion. Mr. Goodwin takes your bag, by
force if necessary, and examines its contents. If you com-
plain, we are two to one. Sit down, madam."

"This is contemptible!"

"No. It's our justifiable reaction to your attempt to
humbug us. You are not under duress, but if you go you

leave your name behind. Sit down and we'll discuss it, but first the name."

She may have been over-optimistic to think she could breeze into Nero Wolfe's office and fool him, but she wasn't a fool. She stood surveying the situation, all signs of nervousness gone, came to a conclusion, opened her bag, and got out an object which she displayed to Wolfe. "My driving license."

He took it and gave it a look and handed it back to her, and she seated herself. "I'm Laura Fromm," she said, "Mrs. Damon Fromm. I am a widow. My New York residence is at Seven-forty-three East Sixty-eighth Street. Tuesday, driving a car on Thirty-fifth Street, I told a boy to get a cop. I gathered from your advertisement that you can direct me to the boy, and I will pay you for it."

"So you don't admit this is an imposture."

"Certainly not."

"What time of day was it?"

"That's not important."

"What was the boy doing when you spoke to him?"

"Neither is that."

"How far away was the boy when you spoke to him, and how loudly did you shout?"

She shook her head. "I'm not going to answer any questions about it. Why should I?"

"But you maintain that you were driving the car and told the boy to get a cop?"

"Yes."

"Then you're in a pickle. The police want to question you about a murder. On Wednesday a car ran over the boy and killed him. Intentionally."

She gawked. "What?"

"It was the same car. The one you were driving Tuesday when the boy spoke to you."

She opened her mouth and closed it. Then she got words out. "I don't believe it."

"You will. The police will explain to you how they know it was the same car. There's no question about it, Mrs. Fromm."

"I mean the whole thing—you're making it up. This is—worse than contemptible."

Wolfe's head moved. "Archie, get yesterday's *Times*."

I went for it to the shelf where the papers are kept until they're a week old. Opening it to page eight and folding it, I crossed and handed it to Laura Fromm. Her hand was shaking a little as she took it, and to steady it while she read she called on the other hand to help hold it.

She took plenty of time for the reading. When her eyes lifted, Wolfe said, "There is nothing there to indicate that Peter Drossos was the boy you had accosted on Tuesday, but you don't need to take my word for that. The police will tell you about it."

Her eyes darted back and forth, from Wolfe to me and back again, and then settled on me. "I want—could I have some gin?"

She had let the newspaper drop to the floor. I picked it up and asked, "Straight?"

"That will do. Or a Gibson?"

"Onion?"

"No. No, thank you. But double?"

I went to the kitchen for the ingredients and ice. As I stirred I was thinking that if she was hoping for any cooperation from Wolfe it was too bad she had asked for gin, since in his book all gin drinkers were barbarians. That was probably why, when I took the tray in and put it on the little table beside her chair, he was leaning back with his eyes closed. I poured and served. First she swigged it, then had a few sips, and then swigged again. Meanwhile she kept her eyes lowered, presumably to keep me from looking in through them to watch her mind work.

Finally she emptied the glass the second time, put it on the tray and spoke. "A man was driving the car when it struck the boy."

Wolfe opened his eyes. "The tray, Archie?"

The smell of gin, especially with lunch only half an hour away, was of course repulsive. I took the vile object to the kitchen and returned.

". . . but though that isn't conclusive," Wolfe was saying, "since in a man's clothes you could pass for a man if you avoided scrutiny, I admit it is relevant. Anyhow, I am not assuming that you killed the boy. I tell you merely that by being drawn to me by that advertisement, and coming rigged in those earrings and that bogus scratch, you have put your foot in it, and if you stick to it that you were

driving that car on Tuesday you will have fully qualified as
a feeble-minded donkey."

"I wasn't."

"That's better. Where were you Tuesday afternoon from
six-thirty to seven?"

"At a meeting of the Executive Committee of the Association for the Aid of Displaced Persons. It lasted until
after seven. It was one of the causes my husband was interested in, and I am going on with it."

"Where were you Wednesday afternoon from six-thirty
to seven?"

"What has that—oh. The boy was—yes. That was day
before yesterday." She paused, not for long. "I was having
cocktails at the Churchill with a friend."

"The friend's name, please?"

"This is ridiculous."

"I know it is. Almost as ridiculous as that scratch on your
cheek."

"The friend's name is Dennis Horan. A lawyer."

Wolfe nodded. "Even so you are in for some disagreeable
hours. I doubt if you have been willfully implicated in murder. I have had some experience watching faces, and I don't
think your shock on hearing of the boy's death was feigned;
but you'd better get your mind arranged. You're going to
get it. Not from me. I don't ask why you tried this mas-
querade, because I'm not concerned, but the police will be
insistent about it. I won't attempt to hold you here for
them; you may go. You will hear from them."

Her eyes were brighter and her chin was higher. It
doesn't take gin long to get in a kick. "I don't have to
hear from them," she said with assurance. "Why do I?"

"Because they'll want to know why you came here."

"I mean why do you have to tell them?"

"Because I withhold information pertinent to a crime
only under dictation by my interest."

"I haven't committed any crime."

"That's what they'll want you to establish, but that won't
satisfy their curiosity."

She looked at me, and I returned it. I may not be a Nero
Wolfe at reading faces, but I too have had some experience at it, and I swear she was sizing me up, trying to
decide if there was any way of lining me up with her in

case she told Wolfe to go sit on a tack. I made it easy for
her by looking manly, staunch and virtuous, but not actually hostile. I saw it on her face when she gave me up.
Leaving me as hopeless, she opened the green suede bag,
took from it a leather fold and a pen, opened the fold on
the little table, and bent over it to write. Having written,
she tore a small blue rectangle of paper from the fold and
left her chair to put it in front of Wolfe on his desk.

"That's a check for ten thousand dollars," she told him.

"I see it is."

"It's a retainer."

"For what?"

"Oh, I'm not trying to bribe you." She smiled. It was the
first time she had shown any reaction resembling a smile,
and I gave her a mark for it. "It looks as if I'm going to
need some expert advice, and maybe some expert help, and
you already know about it, and I wouldn't want—I don't
care to consult my lawyer, at least not now."

"Bosh. You're offering to pay me not to tell the police
of your visit."

"No, I'm not." Her eyes were shining but not soft. "All
right, I am, but not objectionably. I am Mrs. Damon
Fromm. My husband left me a large fortune, including a
great deal of New York real estate. I have position and re-
sponsibilities. If you report this to the police I would
arrange to see the Commissioner, and I don't think I would
be abused, but I would much rather not. If you'll come to
my home at noon tomorrow, I'll know what—"

"I don't go to people's homes."

"Oh yes, you don't." She frowned, but only for an instant. "Then I'll come here."

"At noon tomorrow?"

"No, if it's here, eleven-thirty would be better because I
have a one-o'clock appointment. Until then you will not
report my coming today. I want to—I must see someone. I
must try to find out something. Tomorrow I will tell you
all about it—no, I won't say that. I'll say this: if I don't tell
you all about it tomorrow you will inform the police if you
decide you have to. If I do tell you I will need your advice
and I will probably need your help. That's what the retainer
is for."

Wolfe grunted. His head turned. "Archie. Is she Mrs. Damon Fromm?"

"I would say yes, but I won't sign it."

He went to her. "Madam, you tried one imposture and abandoned it only under pressure; this could be another. Mr. Goodwin will go to a newspaper office and look at pictures of Mrs. Damon Fromm, and phone me from there. Half an hour should do it. You will stay here with me."

She smiled again. "This *is* ridiculous."

"No doubt. But under the circumstances, not unreasonable. Do you refuse?"

"Of course not. I suppose I deserve it."

"You don't object?"

"No."

"Then it isn't necessary. You are Mrs. Fromm. Before you leave, an understanding and a question. The understanding: my decision whether to accept your retainer and work for you will be made tomorrow; you are not now my client. The question: do you know who the woman was who drove that car Tuesday and spoke to the boy?"

She shook her head. "Make your decision tomorrow, that's all right, but you won't report this visit before then?"

"No. That's understood. The question?"

"I'm not going to answer it now because I can't. I don't really know. I expect to answer it tomorrow."

"But you think you know?" Wolfe insisted.

"I won't answer it."

He frowned at her. "Mrs. Fromm. I must warn you. Have you ever seen or heard of a man named Matthew Birch?"

She frowned back. "No. Birch? No. Why?"

"A man of that name was run over by a car and killed Tuesday evening, and it was the same car as the one that killed Peter Drossos Wednesday. Since the car itself cannot be supposed ruthless and malign, someone associated with it must be. I am warning you not to be foolhardy, or even imprudent. You have told me next to nothing, so I don't know how imminent or deadly a doom you may be inviting, but I admonish you: beware!"

"The same car? Killed a man Tuesday?"

"Yes. Since you didn't know him you are not concerned, but I urge you to be discreet."

She sat frowning, "I am discreet, Mr. Wolfe."

"Not today, with that silly sham."

"Oh, you're wrong! I was being discreet! Or trying to." She got the leather fold and pen from the table, returned them to her bag, and closed it. She stood up. "Thank you for the gin, but I wish I hadn't asked for it. I shouldn't have." She offered a hand.

Wolfe doesn't usually rise when a woman enters or leaves the office. That time he did, but it was no special tribute to Laura Fromm or even to the check she had put on his desk. It was lunchtime, and he would have had to manipulate his bulk in a minute anyway. So he was on his feet to take her hand. Of course I was up, ready to take her to the door, and I thought it was darned gracious of her to give me a hand too, after the way I had repulsed her with my incorruptible look. I nearly bumped into her when, preceding me to the door, she suddenly turned to say to Wolfe, "I forgot to ask. The boy, Peter Drossos, was he a displaced person?"

Wolfe said he didn't know.

"Could you find out? And tell me tomorrow?"

He said he could.

There was no car waiting for her in front. Apparently the parking situation had compelled even Mrs. Damon Fromm to resort to taxis. When I returned to the office Wolfe wasn't there, and I found him in the kitchen, lifting the lid from a steaming casserole of lamb cutlets with gammon and tomatoes. It smelled good enough to eat.

"One thing I admit," I said generously. "You have damn good eyes. But of course pretty women's faces are so irresistible to you that you resented the scratch and so you focused on it."

He ignored it. "Are you going to the bank after lunch to deposit Mr. Corliss's check?"

"You know I am."

"Go also to Mrs. Fromm's bank and have her check certified. That will verify her signature. Fritz, this is even better than last time. Satisfactory."

5 Before noon the next day, Saturday, I had plenty of dope on our prospective client. To begin with, five minutes spent in the *Gazette* morgue, by courtesy of my friend Lon Cohen, settled it that she was Mrs. Damon Fromm. She was good for somewhere between five million and twenty million, and since it was unlikely that we would ever want to bill her for more than a million or two, I·didn't go any further into that. Her husband, who had been about twice her age, had died two years ago of a heart attack, leaving her the works. No children. She was born Laura Atherton, of a Philadelphia family of solid citizens, and had been married to Fromm seven years when he died.

Fromm had inherited a small pile and had built it into a mountain, chiefly in the chemical industry. His contributions to various organizations had caused an assortment of chairmen and chairladies and executive secretaries, upon news of his death, to have a deep and decent interest in the terms of his will, but except for a few modest bequests everything had gone to his widow. However, she had carried on with the contributions, and had also been generous with her time and energy, with special attention to Assadip, which was the cable code for the Association for the Aid of Displaced Persons, and the way it was usually spoken of by people who were thrifty with their breath.

If I give the impression that I had spent many hours on a thorough job of research, I should correct it. A quarter of an hour with Lon Cohen, after consulting the *Gazette's* morgue, gave me all of the above except one item, which I got at our bank. There was no danger of Lon blatting around that Nero Wolfe was getting briefed on Mrs. Damon Fromm, since we had given him at least as many breaks on stories as he had given us on scuttlebutt.

At a quarter to twelve Saturday morning Wolfe was at his desk and I was standing at his elbow, rechecking with him the expense account of the job for Corliss (not his name), the hardware manufacturer (not his line). Wolfe thought he had found a twenty-dollar error in it, and it was up to me to prove he was wrong. It turned out to be a draw. Twenty dollars that I had charged against Orrie Cather should have been charged against Saul Panzer, which put me one down, but that made no difference in the grand total, which made us even. As I gathered up the sheets and crossed to the filing cabinet I glanced at my wrist. One minute to twelve.

"Twenty-nine minutes after eleven-thirty," I remarked. "Shall I phone her?"

He muttered no, and I went to the safe for the checkbook, to take care of some household bills, while Wolfe flipped the radio switch at his desk for the twelve-o'clock news. As I sat filling in the stubs my ears heard and I half listened:

"The coming Bermuda conference of the leaders of the United States, Great Britain, and France, which has been rendered somewhat doubtful by the fall of Premier Mayer, will probably be proceeded with as arranged. It is thought that Mayer's successor will be established in office in time to take the third place at the table.

"There is speculation in Tokyo that the three-day interval in the Korean truce negotiations granted at the request of the United Nations Command was intended to permit further consultation among representatives of the United Nations powers in the United States and at the Tokyo headquarters of General Mark W. Clark, the United Nations commander.

"The body of Mrs. Damon Fromm, wealthy New York socialite and philanthropist, was found early today lying in a passage between pillars of the East Side elevated highway now under construction. According to the police, she had been run over by a car, and it is not believed to have been an accident.

"An estimated million and a quarter New Yorkers got an impressive capsule demonstration of the might of American armed forces . . ."

Wolfe didn't turn it off. As far as I could tell from his

expression, he was actually listening. But by the time the five minutes were up he was developing a scowl, and after flipping the switch he let it have his face without restraint.

"So," I said.

There were a dozen comments that could have been made, but none would have helped any. Wolfe certainly didn't need to be reminded that he had warned her not to be foolhardy or even imprudent. Also his scowl did not encourage comment. After a little he placed his palms on the arms of his chair and slowly moved them back and forth, rubbing the rough tapestry with a swishing sound. That went on for a while, then he folded his arms and sat straight.

"Archie."

"Yes, sir."

"How long will it take you to type an account of our conversation with Mrs. Fromm? Not verbatim. With your superlative memory you could come close to it, but that isn't necessary. Just the substance, adequately, as you would report to me."

"You could dictate it."

"I'm in no humor for dictation."

"Leave out anything?"

"Include only what is significant. Do not include my telling her that the same car killed Peter Drossos and Matthew Birch, since that has not been published."

"Twenty minutes."

"Type it in the form of a statement to be signed by you and me. Two carbons. Date it twelve noon today. You will take the original to Mr. Cramer's office immediately."

"Half an hour. For a signed statement I'll want to take more care."

"Very well."

I exceeded my estimate by less than five minutes. It covered three pages, and Wolfe read each page as it was finished. He made no corrections, and even no remarks, which was even stronger evidence of his state of mind than his refusal to dictate. We both signed it, and I stuck it in an envelope.

"Cramer won't be there," I told him. "Neither will Stebbins. Not with this to work on."

He said anyone would do, and I went.

I'm not a stranger at the Tenth Precinct on West 20th Street, which includes the headquarters of Manhattan Homicide West, but that day I saw no familiar faces until I mounted to the second floor and approached one at a desk with whom I was on speaking terms. I had been right; no Cramer and no Stebbins. Lieutenant Rowcliff was in charge, and the desk man phoned that I was there to see him.

If there were twenty of us, including Rowcliff, starving on an island, and we were balloting to elect the one we would carve up for a barbecue, I wouldn't vote for Rowcliff because I know I couldn't keep him down; and compared to his opinion of me, mine of him is sympathetic. So I wasn't surprised when, instead of having me conducted within, he came striding out and up to me, and rasped, "What do you want?"

I took the envelope from my pocket. "This," I said, "is not my application for a job on the force so I can serve under you."

"By God, if it were." He talked like that.

"Nor is it a citation—"

He jerked the envelope from my hand, removed the contents, darted a glance at the heading, turned to the third page, and darted another at the signatures,

"A statement by you and Wolfe. A masterpiece, no doubt. Do you want a receipt?"

"Not necessarily. I'll read it to you if you want me to."

"All I want of you is the sight of your back on the way out."

But without waiting for what he wanted, he wheeled and strode off. I told the one at the desk, "Kindly note that I delivered that envelope to that baboon at one-six Daylight Saving," and departed.

Back at the house, Wolfe had just started lunch, and I joined him in the operation on an anchovy omelet. He permits no talk of business at meals, and interruptions are out of the question, so it was further evidence of his state of mind when, as he was working on a fig and cherry tart, the phone ringing took me to the office, and I returned and told him, "A man named Dennis Horan on the line. You may remem—"

"Yes. What does he want?"

"You."

"We'll call him back in ten minutes."

"He's going places and won't be available."

He didn't even confound it. He didn't hustle any, but he went. I did too, and was at the phone at my desk before he reached his. He sat and got it to his ear.

"Nero Wolfe speaking."

"I'm Dennis Horan, Mr. Wolfe, counselor-at-law. There has been a terrible tragedy. Mrs. Damon Fromm is dead. Run over by a car."

"Indeed. When?"

"The body was found at five'clock this morning." His voice was a thin tenor that seemed to want to squeak, but that could have been from the shock of the tragedy. "I was a friend of hers and handled some matters for her, and I'm calling about the check she gave you yesterday for ten thousand dollars. Has it been deposited?"

"No."

"That's good. Since she is dead of course it won't go through. Do you wish to mail it to her home address, or would you prefer to send it to me?"

"Neither. I'll deposit it."

"But it won't go through! Outstanding checks signed by a deceased person are not—"

"I know. It is certified. It was certified at her bank yesterday afternoon."

"Oh." A fairly long pause. "But since she is dead and can't use your services, since you can do nothing for her, I don't see how you can claim—I mean, wouldn't it be proper and ethical for you to return the check?"

"You are not my mentor in propriety and ethics, Mr. Horan."

"I don't say I am. But without any animus or prejudice, I put it to you, under the circumstances how can you justify keeping that money?"

"By earning it."

"You intend to earn it?"

"I do."

"How?"

"That's my affair. If you are an accredited representative of Mrs. Fromm's estate I am willing to discuss it with you, but not now on the telephone. I'll be available here at my office from now until four o'clock, or from six to seven, or from nine in the evening until midnight."

"I don't know—I don't believe—I'll see."

He hung up. So did we. Back in the dining room Wolfe finished his tart and his coffee in silence. I waited until we had returned to the office and he was adjusted in his chair to remark, "Earning it would be fine, but the main thing is to feel you've earned it. No animus, but I doubt if delivering that statement to Rowcliff is quite enough. My ego is itching."

"Deposit the check," he muttered.

"Yes, sir."

"We need information."

"Yes, sir."

"See Mr. Cohen and get it."

"About what?"

"Everything. Include Matthew Birch, with the understanding that his knowledge of that connection is not to be disclosed unless the police release it or he gets it from some other source. Tell him nothing. It may be published that I am engaged on the case, but not the source of my interest."

"Do I tell him that Pete came to see you?"

"No."

"He would appreciate it. It would be an exclusive human interest story for him. Also it would show that your reputation—"

His fist hit the desk, which for him was a convulsion. "No!" he roared. "Reputation? Am I to invite the comment that it is a mortal hazard to solicit my help? On Tuesday, that boy. On Friday, that woman. They are both dead. I will not have my office converted into an anteroom for the morgue!"

"Yeah. Something of the sort had occurred to me."

"You were well advised not to voice it. The person responsible would have been well advised not to induce it. We will need Saul and Fred and Orrie, but I'll attend to that. Go."

I did so. I took a taxi to the *Gazette* office. The receptionist on the third floor, who had not only received me before but also had been, for three or four years, on the list of those who receive a box of orchids from Wolfe's

plant rooms twice a year, spoke to Lon on the intercom and
waved me in.

I don't know what Lon Cohen is on the *Gazette* and
I doubt if he does. City or wire, daily or Sunday, foreign
or national or local, he seems to know his way in and
around without ever having to work at it. His is the only
desk in a room about nine by twelve, and that's just as well
because otherwise there would be no place for his feet,
which are also about nine by twelve. From the ankles up he
is fairly regular.

There were two colleagues in with him when I entered,
but they soon finished and went. As we shook he said, "Stay
on your feet. You can have two minutes."

"Nuts. An hour may do it."

"Not today. We're spinning on the Fromm murder. The
only reason you got in at all, I want your release on the item
that Nero Wolfe was making inquiries yesterday about Mrs.
Fromm."

"I don't think—" I let it hang while I moved a chair and
sat. "No, better not. But okay on an item that he is working
on the murder."

"He is?"

"Yep."

"Who hired him?"

I shook my head. "It came by carrier pigeon, and he
won't tell me."

"Take off your shoes and socks while I light a cigarette. A
few applications to your tender flesh should do it. I want
the name of the client."

"J. Edgar Hoover."

He made an unseemly noise. "Just a whisper, to me?"

"No."

"But it's open that Wolfe is working on the Fromm
murder?"

"Yes. Just that."

"And the boy, Peter Drossos? And Matthew Birch?
Them too?"

I gave him a look. "How come?"

"Oh, for God's sake. Wolfe's ad in the *Times* wanting to
date a woman wearing spider earrings who had asked a boy
at Ninth Avenue and Thirty-fifth Street to get a cop. Mrs.
Fromm was wearing spider earrings, and you were here

yesterday asking about her. As for Birch, the pattern. His body was found in a secluded spot, flattened by a car, and so was Mrs. Fromm's. I repeat the question."

"I answer it. Nero Wolfe is investigating the murder of Mrs. Fromm with his accustomed vigor, skill, and laziness. He will not rest until he gets the bastard or until bedtime, whichever comes first. Any mention you make of other murders should come on another page."

"No connection implied?"

"Not by him or me. If I should ask for information on Birch, it will be because you dragged him in yourself."

"Okay, hold everything. I want to catch the early."

He left the room. I sat and tried to argue Wolfe into letting Lon have the juicy item about the flap from Matthew Birch's pocket being found on the car that had killed Pete, but since Wolfe wasn't there I made no progress. Before long Lon came back, and after he had crossed to his desk and got his big feet under it I told him, "I still need an hour."

"We'll see. There's not much nourishment in that crumb."

It didn't take a full hour, but a big hunk of one. He gave me nearly everything I wanted without consulting any documents and with only two phone calls to shopmates.

Mrs. Fromm had had lunch Friday at the Churchill with Miss Angela Wright, Executive Secretary of Assadip—the Association for the Aid of Displaced Persons. Presumably she had gone to the Churchill upon leaving Wolfe's office, but I didn't go into that with Lon. After lunch, around two-thirty, the two women had gone together to the office of Assadip, where Mrs. Fromm signed some papers and made some phone calls. The Gazette didn't have her taped from around 3:15 to around five, when she had returned to her home on Sixty-eighth Street and had spent an hour or so working with her personal secretary, Miss Jean Estey. According to Lon, Angela Wright was a credit to her sex, since she would talk to reporters, and Jean Estey wasn't, since she wouldn't.

A little before seven o'clock Mrs. Fromm had left home, alone, to go out to dinner, driving one of her cars, a Cadillac convertible. The dinner was at the apartment of Mr. and Mrs. Dennis Horan on Gramercy Park. It wasn't known

where she had parked the car, but in that neighborhood in
the evening there are always spaces. There had been six
people at the dinner:

> Dennis Horan, the host
> Claire Horan, his wife
> Laura Fromm
> Angela Wright
> Paul Kuffner, public-relations expert
> Vincent Lipscomb, magazine publisher

The party had broken up a little after eleven, and the
guests had gone their ways separately. Mrs. Fromm had
been the last to leave. The *Gazette* had a tip that Horan
had taken her down to her car, but the police weren't
saying, and it couldn't be checked. That was all on Laura
Fromm until five o'clock Saturday morning, when a man
on his way to work in a fish market, passing through the
construction lane between the pillars, had found the body.

Just a few minutes before I reached the *Gazette* office
the District Attorney had announced that Mrs. Fromm had
been run over by her own car. The convertible had been
found parked on Sixteenth Street between Sixth and
Seventh Avenues, only a five-minute walk from the Tenth
Precinct, and had yielded not only evidence of that fact
but also a heavy tire wrench, found on the floor, which had
been used on the back of Mrs. Fromm's head. Whether
the murderer had been concealed in the car, under a rug
behind the front seat, when Mrs. Fromm had come down
to it, or whether he had been allowed by her to get in with
her, then or later, it seemed better than a guess that he
had picked a moment and spot to hit her with the wrench,
replace her at the wheel, drive to an appropriate site, un-
occupied and unobserved at that hour, unload her, and run
the car over her. It would have been interesting and instruc-
tive to go down to Centre Street and watch the scientists
working on that car, but they wouldn't have let me get
within a mile of it, and anyhow I was busy with Lon.

As far as the *Gazette* knew, as of that moment the field
was wide open, with no candidate favored either by the
police or by any outside talent. Of course those who had

been present at the dinner were in a glare, but it could have been anyone who had known where Mrs. Fromm would be, or even possibly someone who hadn't. Lon had no suggestions to offer, though he tossed in the comment that one *Gazette* female was being curious about Mrs. Horan's attitude toward the progress of the friendship between her husband and Mrs. Fromm.

I made an objection. "But if you want to fit in Pete Drossos and Matthew Birch, that's no good. Unless you can make it good. Who was Matthew Birch?"

Lon snorted. "On your way out buy a Wednesday *Gazette*."

"I've got one at home and I've read it. But that was three days ago."

"He hasn't changed any. He was a special agent of the Immigration and Naturalization Service, had been for twenty years, with a wife and three children. He had only twenty-one teeth, looked like a careworn statesman, dressed beyond his station, wasn't any too popular in his circle, and bet on the races through Danny Pincus."

"You said you counted Birch in because of the pattern. Was there any other reason?"

"No."

"Just to your old and trusted friend Goodwin. Any at all?"

"No."

"Then I'll do you a favor, expecting it back with interest at your earliest convenience. It's triple classified. The cops have it sewed up that the car that killed Pete Drossos was the one that killed Birch."

His eyes widened. "No!"

"Yes."

"Sewed up how?"

"Sorry, I've forgotten. But it's absolutely tight."

"I'll be damned." Lon rubbed his palms together. "This is sweet, Archie. This is very sweet. Pete and Mrs. Fromm, the earrings. Pete and Birch, the car. That ties Birch and Mrs. Fromm. You understand that the *Gazette* will now have a strong hunch that the three murders are connected and will proceed accordingly."

"As long as it's just a hunch, okay."

"Right. As for the car itself—as you know, the license plate was a floater; the car was stolen in Baltimore four months ago. It's been repainted twice."

"That hasn't been published."

"They released it at noon." Lon leaned to me. "Listen, I've got an idea. How can you be absolutely sure I'm to be trusted unless you try me? Here's your chance. Tell me how they know the same car killed Birch and the boy. Then I'll forget it."

"I forgot it first." I stood up and shook my pants legs down. "My God, are you a glutton! Dogs should be fed once a day, and you've had yours."

6

When I got back to Thirty-fifth Street it was after four o'clock and the office was empty. I went to the kitchen to ask Fritz if there had been any visitors, and he said yes, Inspector Cramer.

I raised my brows. "Any blood flow?"

He said no, but it had been pretty noisy. I treated myself to a tall glass of water, returned to the office, and buzzed the plant rooms on the house phone, and when Wolfe answered I told him, "Home again. Regards from Lon Cohen. Do I type the report?"

"No. Come up and tell me."

That was not exactly busting a rule, like the interruption at lunch, but it was exceptional. It suited me all right, since as long as he stayed sore because he thought someone had made a monkey of him he would probably make his brain work. I went up the three flights and through the aluminum door into the vestibule, and the door to the warm room, where the Miltonia roezli and Phalaenopsis Aphrodite were in full bloom. In the next room, the medium, only a few of the big show-offs, the Cattleyas and Laelias, had flowers, which was all right with me, and anyway the biggest show-off in the place, named Wolfe, was there, helping Theodore adjust the muslin shaders. When I appeared he led the way to the rear, through the cool room into the potting room, where he lowered himself into the only chair present and demanded, "Well?"

I got onto a stool and gave it to him. He sat with his eyes closed and his nose twitching now and then for punctuation. In making a report to him one of my objectives is to cover it so well as I go along that at the end he won't have one question to ask, and that time I made it. When I had finished he held his pose a long moment, then opened his eyes and informed me, "Mr. Cramer was here."

I nodded. "So Fritz said. He also said it was noisy."

"Yes. He was uncommonly offensive. Of course he is under harassment, but so am I. He intimated that if I had told him yesterday of Mrs. Fromm's visit she would not have been killed, which is poppycock. Also he threatened me. If I obstruct the police investigation in any way I will be summoned. Pfui! Is he still downstairs?"

"Not unless he's hiding in the bathroom. Fritz said he left."

"I left him and came up here. I have phoned Saul and Fred and Orrie. What time is it?"

He would have had to turn his head to see the clock, so I told him. "Ten to five."

"They will be here at six or soon after. There has been no word from Mr. Horan. How old is Jean Estey?"

"Lon didn't specify, but he said young, so I suppose not over thirty. Why?"

"Is she comely?"

"No data."

"You have a right to know. At any rate, she is young. Saul or Fred or Orrie may find a crack for us, but I don't want to prowl around this cage while they try. I want to know what Mrs. Fromm did from three-fifteen to five o'clock yesterday afternoon, and what and whom her mind was on during the hour she spent with Miss Estey. Miss Estey can tell me—certainly the second, and probably the first. Get her and bring her here."

Don't misunderstand him. He knew it was fantastic. He hadn't the slightest expectation that under the circumstances I could get to Mrs. Fromm's personal secretary for a private chat, let alone convoy her to his office so he could pump her. But it would only cost him some taxi fare, so what the hell, why not let me stub my toe on the slim chance that I might raise some dust?

So I merely remarked that I would tell Fritz to set an extra place for dinner in case she was hungry, left him, went down one flight to my bedroom, stood by the window, and surveyed the problem. In ten minutes I concocted, and rejected, four different plans. The fifth one seemed more likely, at least with a faint chance of working, and I voted for it. For dressing the part nothing in my personal wardrobe would do, so I went to the closet where I kept an assortment of items for professional emergencies such as the present and got out a black cutaway and vest, striped trousers, a white shirt with starched collar, a black Homburg, and a black four-in-hand. Suitable shoes and socks were in my personal stock. When I had shaved and got into the costume I took a look in the full-length mirror and was impressed. All I needed was either a bride or a hearse.

Downstairs in the office I got a little Marley .22 from the collection in a drawer of my desk, loaded it, and stuck it in my hip pocket. That was a compromise. A shoulder holster with a .32 would have spoiled my contours in that getup, but long ago, after a couple of unpleasant experiences, one of which had made it necessary to have a bullet dug out of my chest, I had promised both Wolfe and myself that I would never go forth unarmed to deal with anyone involved in a murder, however remotely. That attended to, I went to the kitchen to give Fritz a treat.

"I've been appointed," I told him, "ambassador to Texas. Adieu."

He asked me to unbutton the shirt to show him my girdle.

It was 5:38 when I paid the taxi driver in front of the address on East Sixty-eighth Street. Across the street there was a little assembly of gawkers, but on this side a uniformed cop was keeping the citizens moving. The house was granite, set back a couple of yards, with iron railings higher than my head protecting the areaway on both sides of the entrance. As I headed for it the cop moved to meet me, but not actually to block me. Cops prefer not to block personages dressed as I was.

I stopped, looked at him mournfully, and said, "Arrangements."

He might have made it more difficult by accompanying me to the door, but three female sightseers gave me an assist just then by converging on the iron railing, and by the time he had persuaded them on their way I had entered the vestibule, pushed the button, and was speaking to a specimen with an aristocratic nose who had opened the door. His color scheme was the same as mine, but I had it on him in style.

"There has developed," I said sadly but firmly, "some confusion in the directions about the flowers, and it must be settled. I will have to see Miss Estey."

Since it would have been out of character to slide a foot across the sill against the open door I had to keep that impulse down, but when he opened it enough to give me room I lost no time in slipping past him. As he closed the door I remarked, "The morbid curiosity of the public at such a time is distressing. Will you please tell Miss Estey that Mr. Goodwin would like to consult her about the flowers?"

"This way, please."

He led me five paces along the hall to a door that was standing open, motioned me in, and told me to wait. The room was nothing like what I would have expected in the town residence of Mrs. Damon Fromm. It was smaller than my bedroom, and, in addition to two desks, two typewriter stands, and an assortment of chairs, it was crammed with filing cabinets and miscellaneous objects. The walls were covered with posters and photographs, some framed and some not. There were scores of them. After a general survey I focused on one item and then another, and was inspecting one inscribed, AMERICAN HEALTH COUNCIL, 1947, when I heard footsteps and straightened and turned.

She came in, stopped, and leveled greenish-brown eyes at me. "What's this about flowers?" she demanded.

The eyes didn't look as if they had been irritated by any great flood of tears, but they certainly were not merry. I might possibly have classed her under thirty in happier circumstances, but not as she was then. Comely, yes. She

was not wearing earrings. There was no sign of a scratch
on her cheek, but four days had passed since Pete had
seen it, and he had given no specifications as to depth or
outline. So there wasn't much hope of spotting any vestige
of that scratch on Jean Estey or anyone else.

"Are you Miss Jean Estey?" I asked.

"Yes. What about flowers?"

"That's what I came to tell you. You may have heard
the name Nero Wolfe."

"The detective?"

"Yes."

"Certainly."

"Good. He sent me. My name is Archie Goodwin, and
I work for him. He wants to send flowers to Mrs. Fromm's
funeral, and would like to know if there would be any
objection to orchids, provided they are sprays of Miltonia
roezli alba, which are pure white and are very beautiful."

She stared at me a second and then suddenly burst out
laughing. It wasn't musical. Her shoulders were shaking
with it, and she half walked and half stumbled to a chair,
sat, lowered her head, and pressed her palms against her
temples. The butler came to the threshold of the open
door for a look, and I went to him and told him sympathetically that I had had experience with such crises, which
was no lie, and that it might be well to shut the door. He
agreed and pulled it shut himself. Then for a little I
thought I might have to shock her out of it, but before
long she started to calm down, and I went to a chair and
sat. Soon she came erect and dabbed at her eyes with a
handkerchief.

"What started me," she said, "was the way you're
dressed. It's grotesque—dressed like that to come and ask
if there's any objection to orchids!" She had to stop a
moment to get her breathing in order. "There are to be
no flowers. Now you may go."

"The costume was merely to get me in."

"I understand. Under false pretenses. What for?"

"To see you. Look, Miss Estey. I'm sorry my disguise
brought on that little attack, but now you should sit quietly
for a few minutes while your nerves catch up, and meanwhile why not let me explain? I suppose you know that

Mrs. Fromm came to see Mr. Wolfe yesterday and gave him a check for ten thousand dollars."

"Yes. I handle her personal checking account."

"Did she tell you what it was for?"

"No. All she put on the stub was the word 'retainer.' "

"Well, I can't tell you what it was for, but she was to see Mr. Wolfe again today. The check was certified yesterday and will be deposited Monday. Mr. Wolfe feels a responsibility to Mrs. Fromm and considers that he is obliged to investigate her death."

She was breathing better. "The police are investigating it. Two of them left here just half an hour ago."

"Sure. If they solve it, fine. But if they don't, Mr. Wolfe will. Don't you want him to?"

"It doesn't matter what I want, does it?"

"It matters to Mr. Wolfe. The police can say to anybody involved, 'Answer this one, or else,' but he can't. He wants to talk with you and sent me to bring you to his office, and I can persuade you to come only by one of three methods. I could threaten you if I had a good menace handy, but I haven't. I could bribe you if I knew what to use for bait, but I don't. All that's left is to say that Mrs .Fromm came to see him and gave him that check, and he has reason to think that her death was connected with the matter she hired him to work on and therefore he feels obliged to investigate it, and he wants to start by talking with you. The question is whether you want to help. Naturally I should think you would, without any threats or bribes, even if I had some in stock. Our office is on Thirty-fifth Street. The cop out front will flag a taxi for us, and we can be there in fifteen minutes."

"You mean go now?"

"Sure."

She shook her head. "I couldn't. I have to—I couldn't." She was back in control, with all signs of the attack gone. "You say the question is whether I want to help, but that's not it, it's how I can help." She hesitated, studying me. "I think I'll tell you something."

"I'd appreciate it."

"I told you two policemen, detectives, left here half an hour ago."

"Yes."

"Well, while they were here, not long before they left, there was a phone call for one of them, and after he hung up he said I might be contacted by Nero Wolfe, probably through his assistant, Archie Goodwin, and I might be asked to go to see Nero Wolfe, and if so he hoped I would cooperate by going and then tell the police exactly what Wolfe said."

"That's interesting. Did you agree to cooperate?"

"No. I didn't commit myself." She got up, went to a desk, got a pack of cigarettes from a drawer, lit one, and took two healthy drags. She stood looking down at me. "The reason I told you that is purely selfish. I happen to think that Nero Wolfe is smarter than any policeman, but whether he is or not, Mrs. Fromm went to consult him yesterday and gave him that check, and I don't know what for. Since I'm her secretary of course I'm involved in this, I can't help that, but I'm not going to do anything to get more involved, and I certainly would be if I went to see Nero Wolfe. If I didn't tell the police what Wolfe said they would never let up on me, and if I did tell them —what if he asked me about something that Mrs. Fromm had told him confidentially and wouldn't want the police to know?"

She took another drag at the cigarette, went to a desk and mashed it in a tray, and came back. "So I told you. I'm just a sweet innocent small-town girl from Nebraska, I don't think. If ten years on your own in New York don't teach you how to avoid collisions in heavy traffic, nothing will. Here I am in this mess, but I'm not going to say or do anything to make it worse than it is—for me. I'm going to have to get a job. I don't owe Mrs. Damon Fromm anything—I worked for her, and she paid me, and nothing extravagant, either."

My head was tilted back to look up at her, with my face, if it was obeying orders, earnest and sympathetic. The starched collar was engraving the back of my neck. "You won't get an argument from me, Miss Estey," I assured her. "I've been in New York ten years too, and then some. You say the police wanted you to tell them what Nero Wolfe said, but how about Archie Goodwin? Did they ask you to tell them what I say?"

"I don't think so. No."

"Good. Not that I have anything special to say, but I would like to ask a few questions if you'll sit down."

"I've been sitting answering questions all afternoon."

"I'll bet you have. Such as, where were you last night from ten o'clock to two o'clock?"

She stared. "You're asking me that?"

"No, just giving a sample of the kind of questions you've been answering all afternoon."

"Well, here's a sample of the kind of answers I gave. Yesterday between five and six Mrs. Fromm dictated about a dozen letters. A little after six she went up to dress, and I started on some phone calls she had told me to make. A little after seven, after she had gone out, I had dinner alone, and after dinner I typed the letters she had dictated and went out to mail them at the box at the corner. That was around ten o'clock. I came right back and told Peckham, the butler, I was tired and was going to bed, and went up to my room and turned on WQXR for the music, and went to bed."

"Fine. Then you live here?"

"Yes."

"Another example. Where were you Tuesday afternoon from six o'clock to seven?"

She went and sat down and cocked her head at me. "You're right, they asked me that too. Why?"

I shrugged. "I'm just showing you that I know the kind of questions cops ask."

"You are not. What is it about Tuesday afternoon?"

"First how did you answer it?"

"I couldn't until I thought back. That was the day Mrs. Fromm went to a meeting of the Executive Committee of Assadip—the Association for the Aid of Displaced Persons. She let me take a car—the convertible—and I spent the afternoon and evening chasing all over town trying to find a couple of refugees that Assadip wanted to help. I never found them, and I got home after midnight. I'd have a hard time accounting for every minute of that afternoon and evening, and I don't intend to try. Why should I? What happened Tuesday between six and seven?"

I regarded her. "How about a trade? Tell me where

Mrs. Fromm was yesterday afternoon from three-fifteen to five o'clock, and what letters she dictated from five to six, and what phone calls she made, and I'll tell you what happened Tuesday."

"Those are more samples of what the police asked."

"Naturally. But these I like."

"She made no phone calls at all, but told me to make some later, to ask people to buy tickets for a theater benefit for the Milestone School. There were twenty-three names on the list, and the police have it. The letters she dictated were miscellaneous, just routine matters. Mr. Kuffner and Mr. Horan both said to let the police take the copies, so I did. If you want me to try to remember, I think—"

"Never mind. What did she do between the time she left the Assadip office and the time she got home?"

"I know two things she did. She went to a shop on Madison Avenue and bought some gloves—she brought them home with her—and she called at the office of Paul Kuffner. I don't know whether she did anything else. What happened Tuesday?"

"A car stopped for a light at the corner of Ninth Avenue and Thirty-fifth Street, and the woman driving it told a boy to get a cop."

Her brow wrinkled. "What?"

"I told you."

"But what has that to do with it?"

I shook my head. "Not in the bargain. I said I'd tell you what happened. This is a very complicated business, Miss Estey, and you may decide to tell the police what Archie Goodwin said, and they wouldn't like it if I went around telling the suspects exactly how all the—"

"I'm not a suspect!"

"I beg your pardon. I thought you were. Anyhow, I'm not—"

"Why should I be?"

"If for no other reason, because you were close to Mrs. Fromm and knew where she was last evening and that her car would be parked nearby. But even if you weren't I wouldn't spread it out for you. Mr. Wolfe might feel different. If you change your mind and come down to see him this evening after dinner, or tomorrow morning—say, eleven o'clock, when he'll be free—he might take a notion to empty the bag for you. He's a genius, so you never know. If you—"

The door swinging open stopped me. It swung wide, and a man trotted in. As he appeared he started to say something to Miss Estey, but, becoming aware that she had company, cut it off, stopped short, and proceeded to take me in.

When it seemed that neither was she performing introductions nor was he asking strangers' names, I broke the ice. "My name's Archie Goodwin. I work for Nero Wolfe." Seeing how he was taking me in, I added, "I'm in disguise."

He approached with a hand out, and I arose and took it. "I'm Paul Kuffner."

In size he had been shortchanged, the top of his head being about level with the tip of my nose. With his thin brown mustache trimmed so it wasn't quite parallel with the thick lips of his wide mouth, I wouldn't have called him well designed to make the sort of impression desirable for a handler of public relations, but I admit I'm prejudiced about a mustache trying to pass as a plucked eyebrow.

He smiled at me to show that he liked me, that he approved of everything I had ever said or done, and that he understood all my problems perfectly. "I'm sorry," he said, "that I have to break in like this and take Miss Estey away, but there are some urgent matters. Come upstairs, Miss Estey?"

It was a fine job. Instead of that he could have said, "Get out of this house and give me a chance to ask Miss Estey what the hell you're trying to put over," which was what he meant. But no, sir, he liked me too much to say anything that could possibly hurt my feelings.

When Miss Estey had got up and crossed to the door and passed through, and he had followed her to the sill, he turned to tell me, "It was a pleasure to meet you, Mr. Goodwin. I've heard a great deal about you, and Mr. Wolfe, of course. Sorry our meeting had to be at so difficult a moment." He stepped out of sight, but his voice carried in to me. "Oh, Peckham! Mr. Goodwin's going. See if he wants you to stop a cab for him."

A nice clean fast job. Apparently with that mustache he was in disguise too.

7 I got back to the house in time to hear the briefing. Saul and Orrie were already there, sitting waiting, but Fred hadn't arrived. After greeting them, I reported to Wolfe, who was at his desk.

"I saw her and had a chat with her, but."

"Why the deuce are you arrayed like that?"

"I'm a mortician."

He made a face. "That abominable word. Tell me about it."

I obeyed, giving it in full, but that time he had questions. None of them got him anything, since I had delivered all the facts, and the impression I had got of Jean Estey and Paul Kuffner wasn't any help, even to me, let alone him, and when Saul went to answer the doorbell and brought Fred in, Wolfe dropped me at once and had them move chairs up to a line fronting his desk.

That trio was no great treat to look at. Saul Panzer, with his big nose lording it over his narrow face, in his brown suit that should have been pressed after he got caught in the rain, could have been a hackie or a street sweeper, but he wasn't. He was the smartest operative in the metropolitan area, and his talent for tailing, which Wolfe had praised to Pete Drossos, was only one little part of him. Any agency in town would pay him three times the market.

In bulk Fred Durkin would have made nearly two Sauls, but not in ability. He could tail all right, and you could count on him for any ordinary chore, but if he ran into something fancy he was apt to get twisted. You could trust him to hell and back.

As for Orrie Cather, when he confronted you with his confident dark brown eyes and a satisfied smile on his wavy lips, you had no doubt that his main concern was whether you realized how handsome he was. Of course that irritated any customer he tackled, but it also gave the impression that it wasn't necessary to watch your step, which might be dangerous, since his real concern was his reputation as a working detective.

Wolfe leaned back, rested his forearms on the arms of the chair, drew in a bushel of air, and audibly let it out. "Gentlemen," he said, "I am up to my thighs in a quagmire. Customarily, when I enlist your services, it is enough to define your specific tasks, but this time that won't do. You must be informed of the total situation in all its intricacy, but first a word about money. Less than twelve hours after the client gave me a check for ten thousand dollars, she was murdered. Since no successor to the cliency is in view, that's all I'll get. If it is unavoidable I am prepared, for a personal reason, to spend the major portion, even the entire sum, on the expense of the investigation, but not more. I don't ask you to be niggardly in your expenditures, but I must forbid any prodigality. Now here it is."

Beginning with my ushering Pete Drossos into the dining room Tuesday evening, and ending with my report of my talk with Jean Estey, which Fred had not heard, he went right through it, omitting nothing. They sat absorbing it, each in his manner—Saul slumped and relaxed, Fred stiff and straight, with his eyes fastened on Wolfe as if he had to listen with them too, and Orrie with his temple propped against his fingertips for a studio portrait. As for me, I was trying to catch Wolfe skipping some detail so I would have the pleasure of supplying it when he was through, but nothing doing. I couldn't have done a better job myself.

He glanced up at the clock. "It's twenty past seven, and dinner's ready. We're having fried chicken with cream gravy and mush. We won't discuss this at the table, but I wanted you to have it in your minds."

It was going on nine by the time we were back in the office, having discussed all of five chickens, with accessories, so fully that they were settled for good. Wolfe, after getting arranged in his chair, scowled at me and then at them.

"You don't look very alert," he said peevishly.

They didn't jerk to attention. While none of them had had as much of him as I had, they knew how he hated to work during the hour or so after dinner, and what was eating him wasn't that they weren't alert but that he didn't want to be.

"We can go downstairs," I suggested, "and play some pool while you digest."

He snorted. "My stomach," he asserted, "is quite capable of handling its affairs without pampering. Has any of you gentlemen a pressing question before I go on?"

"Maybe later," Saul suggested.

"Very well. It is, as you see, hopeless. It is excessively complex, but no sources of information are available to us. Archie can try with others as he did with Miss Estey, but he has no lever. The police will tell me nothing. On occasion, in the past, I have had tools wherewith to pry things out of them, but not this time. Since they know everything I know, I have nothing to bargain with. Of course we know presumptively what they're doing. They're finding out, or trying to, whether any woman known to Mrs. Fromm had a scratch on her cheek Tuesday evening or Wednesday. If they find her that could settle it; but they may not find her, since what that boy called a scratch, staring at her as he did, might have been a slight mark that she could have rendered practically unnoticeable as soon as she got a chance. Also the police are trying to find a woman known to Mrs. Fromm who wore spider earrings, and again, if they succeed, that could settle it."

Wolfe upturned a palm. "And they're trying to trace the car that killed the boy and Matthew Birch. They're examining every inch of Mrs. Fromm's car. They're rechecking Birch's movements and connections and associates. They're piecing together, minute by minute, everything Mrs. Fromm did and said after she left this office yesterday. They're badgering not only those who were with Mrs. Fromm last evening, but everyone who can be remotely suspected of knowledge of a pertinent fact. They're checking on the whereabouts of all possible culprits—for Tuesday evening when a woman told Peter Drossos to get a cop, for later that evening when Birch was killed, for Wednesday evening when the boy was killed, and for yesterday evening when Mrs. Fromm was killed. They're asking who had reason to fear or hate Mrs. Fromm or will profit in any way by her death. In those activities they are using a hundred men, or a thousand—all of them trained, and some of them competent."

He compressed his lips and shook his head. "They can't afford to fail on this one, and they won't dally. As we sit here they may have marked their prey and are ready to seize him. But until they do, I propose to use Mrs. Fromm's money or part of it, for a purpose that she would surely have sanctioned. With all their advantages, the police will certainly forestall us, but I intend to persuade myself that I am justified in keeping that money; and besides, I resent the assumption that people who come to me for help can be murdered with impunity. That's the personal reason."

"We'll get the bastard!" Fred Durkin blurted.

"I doubt it, Fred. You understand now why I called you to this conference and told you all about it instead of simply assigning you to errands as usual. I wanted you to know how hopeless it is, and also I wanted to consult you. There are dozens of possible approaches to the problem, and there are only three of you. Saul, where do you think you might start?"

Saul hesitated. He scratched his nose. "I'd like to start two places at once. Assadip and earrings."

"Why Assadip?"

"Because they're interested in displaced persons, and Birch was with the Immigration and Naturalization Service. That's the one chance I see for any connection between Birch and Mrs. Fromm. Of course the cops are on it, but on that kind of trying around anyone might get a lucky break."

"Since Angela Wright, the Executive Secretary of Assadip, was present at the dinner last evening, she is probably unapproachable."

"Not by a displaced person."

"Oh." Wolfe considered. "Yes, you might try that."

"And anyhow, if she's too busy with cops and so on, they must have a couple of stenographers and someone to answer the phone. I'll need a lot of sympathy."

Wolfe nodded. "Very well. In the morning. Take two hundred dollars, but a displaced person would not be lavish. What about earrings?"

"I couldn't do both."

"No, but what about them?"

"Well, I get around some, and I keep my eyes open, but I have never seen spider earrings, either on a woman or in a window. You said that Pete said big gold spiders with their legs stretched out. People would notice that. If she wore them before Tuesday, or after, the cops have already got her spotted or soon will have, and you're probably right, for us it's hopeless. But there's a chance she didn't, and was it the same ones Mrs. Fromm was wearing yesterday? It might pay to try to find some shop that ever sold any spider earrings. The cops are so busy on it from the other angle maybe they haven't started on that. Am I wrong?"

"No. You're seldom wrong. If we find that woman first—"

"I'll take it," Orrie said. "I've never seen any spider earrings either. How big were they?"

"The ones Mrs. Fromm wore yesterday were about the size of your thumbnail—that is, the circumference described by the tips of the extended legs. Archie?"

I responded. "I'd say a little larger."

"Were they gold?"

"I don't know. Archie?"

"My guess is yes, but don't quote me."

"Well made?"

"Yes."

"Okay. I'll take it."

Wolfe was frowning at him. "A month might do it."

"Not the way I'll work it, Mr. Wolfe. I did a favor once for a guy that's a salesman at Boudet's, and I'll start with him. That way I can get going tomorrow even if it is Sunday—I know where he lives. One thing I may have missed —is there any line at all on whether the ones Mrs. Fromm had on yesterday were the same as those the woman in the car was wearing Tuesday?"

"No."

"Then there may be two different pairs?"

"Yes."

"Right. I've got it. Last one across is a rotten egg."

"Will you need to pay your friend, the salesman at Boudet's?"

"Hell, no. He owes me a favor."

"Then take a hundred dollars. If you find anything that offers promise, avoid any hint that the police might be grateful for news of it. We might ourselves find it desirable to bid for official gratitude. At the slightest sign of a trail, phone me." Wolfe transferred to Durkin. "Fred, where do you start?"

Fred's big broad face showed pink. He had done jobs for Wolfe, off and on, for nearly twenty years, and being consulted on high-level strategy was something new to him. He clamped his jaw, swallowed, and said in a much louder voice than was called for, "Them earrings."

"Orrie has the earrings."

"I know he has, but look. Hundreds of people must've seen 'em on her. Elevator men, maids, waiters—"

"No." Wolfe was curt. "In all that area the police are so far ahead that we could never catch up. I have explained that. With our meager forces we must try to find a trail not already explored. Has anyone a suggestion for Fred?"

They exchanged glances. No one volunteered.

Wolfe nodded. "It is certainly difficult. One way to avoid panting along at the heels of the police, with the air polluted by their dust, is to make an assumption that they may not have made, and explore it. Let's try one. I assume that Tuesday afternoon, when the car stopped at the corner and the woman driver told the boy to get a cop, the man in the car with her was Matthew Birch."

Saul frowned. "I don't get it, Mr. Wolfe."

"Good. Then it probably hasn't occurred to the police. I admit it is extremely tenuous. But later that day, that night, that same car ran over Birch and killed him, in a place and manner indicating that it had carried him to the spot. Therefore, since he was in the car late in the evening, why not assume that he was in it early in the evening? I choose so to assume."

Saul maintained his frown. "But the way it stands, wouldn't the assumption be that the man who ran the car over the boy Wednesday was the one who had been with the woman Tuesday? Because he knew the boy could identify him? And on Wednesday Birch was dead."

"That's probably the police assumption," Wolfe conceded. "Its worth is obvious, so I don't reject it; I merely ignore it and substitute one of my own. Even a false assumption may serve a purpose. Columbus assumed that there was nothing but water between him and the treasures of the Orient, and he bumped into a continent." His eyes moved. "I don't expect you to bump into a continent, Fred, but you will proceed on my assumption that Birch was in the car with the woman. Try either to validate it or to disprove it. Take a hundred dollars—no, take three hundred, you never waste money. Archie will supply you with a photograph of Birch." He turned to me. "They should all have photographs of everyone involved. Can you get them from Mr. Cohen?"

"Not tonight. In the morning."

"Do so."

He surveyed his meager forces, left to right and back again. "Gentlemen, I trust I have not dulled your ardor by dwelling on the hopelessness of this enterprise. I wanted you to understand that the situation is such that any titbit will be a feast. I have on occasion expected much of you; this time I expect nothing. It is likely that—"

The doorbell rang.

As I got up and crossed the room I glanced at my wrist. It was 9:55. In the hall, switching on the stoop light and approaching the door, I saw it was two men, both strangers. I opened up and told them good evening.

The one in front spoke. "We want to see Mr. Nero Wolfe."

"Your names, please?"

"Mine is Horan, Dennis Horan. I phoned him this morning. This is Mr. Maddox."

"Mr. Wolfe is busy. I'll see. Step in?"

They entered. I took them into the front room, glanced at the soundproofed door connecting with the office to check that it was closed, invited them to sit, and left them. Going by way of the hall, I shut that door, returned to the office, and told Wolfe, "Two titbits in the front room. One named Horan, who wanted you to cough up the ten grand, with a sidekick named Maddox."

He ran true to form. He glowered at me. Having finished with the briefing, he was all set to relax with a book, and here I was bringing him work to do. If we had been alone he would have indulged in one or two remarks, but after what he had just been telling the squad about hopelessness he had to control it, and I admit he did it like a man.

"Very well. Let Saul and Fred and Orrie out first, after you have given them expense money as specified."

I went to the safe for the dough.

8 From their manner, and glances that passed between them as I ushered the callers into the office and got them into chairs, I gathered that I had been too hasty in assuming they were sidekicks. The glances were not affectionate.

Dennis Horan was a little too much. His eyelashes were a little too long, and he was a little too tall for his width and a little too old for campus tailoring. He needed an expert job of toning down, but since he had apparently spent more than forty years toning up I doubted if he would consider an offer.

Maddox made it plain to Wolfe that his name was James Albert Maddox. He had been suffering with ulcers from the cradle on, close to half a century—or if not, it was up to him to explain how his face had got so sour that looking at him would have turned his own dog into a pessimist. I put them into a couple of the yellow chairs which the boys had vacated, not knowing which of them, if either, rated the red leather one.

Horan opened up. He said that he had not intended, on the phone that morning, to intimate that Wolfe was doing or contemplating anything improper or unethical. He had merely been trying to safeguard the interests of his former friend and client, Mrs. Damon Fromm, who had been—

"Not your client," interposed Maddox in a tone that matched his face perfectly.

"I advised her," Horan snapped.

"Badly," Maddox snapped back.

They regarded each other. Not sidekicks.

"Perhaps," Wolfe suggested dryly, "it would be well for each of you to tell me, without interruption, to what extent and with what authority you represent Mrs. Fromm. Then contradictions can be composed or ignored as may seem desirable. Mr. Horan?"

He was controlling himself. His thin tenor was still thin, but it wasn't as close to a squeak as it had been on the phone. "It is true that I was never Mrs. Fromm's attorney of record in any action. She consulted me in many matters and showed that she valued my advice by frequently acting upon it. As counsel for the Association for the Aid of Displaced Persons, which I still am, I was closely associated with her. If she were alive I don't think she would challenge my right to call myself her friend."

"Are you an executor of her estate?"

"No."

"Thank you. Mr. Maddox?"

It hurt him, but he delivered. "My law firm, Maddox and Welling, was counsel for Damon Fromm for twelve years. Since his death we have been counsel for Mrs. Fromm. I am the executor of her estate. I interrupted because Mr. Horan's statement that Mrs. Fromm was his client was not true. I have something to add."

"Go ahead."

"This morning—no, this afternoon—Mr. Horan phoned and told me of the check Mrs. Fromm gave you yesterday, and of his conversation with you. His call to you was gratuitous and impertinent. My call on you now is not. I ask you formally, as Mrs. Fromm's counsel and executor of her estate, under what arrangement and for what purpose did she give you her check for ten thousand dollars? If you prefer to tell me privately, let us withdraw. Mr. Horan insisted on coming with me, but this is your house, and that young man looks quite capable of dealing with him."

If he intended the glance he shot at me to be complimentary, I'd hate to have him give me one of disapproval.

Wolfe spoke. "I don't prefer to tell you privately, Mr. Maddox. I prefer not to tell you at all."

Maddox didn't look any sourer, because he couldn't. "Do you know law, Mr. Wolfe?"

"No."

"Then you should seek advice. Unless you can establish that Mrs. Fromm received value for that payment, I can compel you to disgorge it. I am giving you a chance to establish it."

"I can't. She received nothing. As I told Mr. Horan on the phone, I intend to earn that money."

"How?"

"By making sure that the murderer of Mrs. Fromm is exposed and punished."

"That's ridiculous. That's the function of officers of the law. The information I got about you today, on inquiry, indicated that you are not a shyster, but you sound like one."

Wolfe chuckled. "You're prejudiced, Mr. Maddox. The feeling of virtuous lawyers toward shysters is the same as that of virtuous women toward prostitutes. Condemnation, certainly; but somewhere in it one tiny grain of envy, not to be recognized, let alone acknowledged. But don't envy me. A shyster is either a fool or a fanatic, and I am neither. I would like to ask a question."

"Ask it."

"Did you know that Mrs. Fromm intended to call on me, before she came?"

"No."

"Did you know that she had called on me, after she came?"

"No."

Wolfe's eyes moved. "You, Mr. Horan? Both questions."

"I don't see—" Horan hesitated. "I question your right to ask them."

Maddox looked at him. "Meet him, Horan. You insisted on coming. You have claimed that Mrs. Fromm consulted you on important matters. He's trying to lay ground. If he can establish that she told either you or me that she was coming to him, or had come, without disclosing what for, he'll take the position that manifestly she didn't want us to know and therefore he can't betray the confidence. Head him off."

Horan wasn't buying it. "I will not," he insisted, "submit to a cross-examination."

Maddox started to argue, but Wolfe cut in. "Your elucidation may be acute as far as it goes, Mr. Maddox, but you don't appreciate Mr. Horan's difficulty. He is stumped. If to my second question he says yes, you're right, I have a weapon and I'll use it. But if he says no, then I ask him how he knew that Mrs. Fromm had given me a check. I'll want to know, and I should think you will too."

"I already know. At least I know what he told me. This morning, when he heard of Mrs. Fromm's death, he telephoned her home and spoke with Miss Estey, Mrs. Fromm's secretary, and she told him about the check. I was in the country for the weekend, and Horan got me there. I drove to town immediately."

"Where in the country?"

Maddox's chin went up. "That's sheer impudence."

Wolfe waved it away. "At any rate, it's futile. I beg your pardon, not for impudence but for stupidity. Force of habit impelled it. In this intricate maze I must leave the conventional procedures, such as inquiry into alibis, to the police. Since you're not stumped, Mr. Horan, will you answer my questions?"

"No. On principle. You have no warrant to ask them."

"But you expect me to answer yours?"

"No, not mine, because I have no warrant either. But Mr. Maddox has, as executor of the estate. You'll answer him."

"We'll see." Wolfe was judicious. He addressed Maddox. "As I understand it, sir, you are not demanding that I return the money Mrs. Fromm paid me."

"That depends. Tell me under what arrangement and for what purpose it was paid, and I'll consider the matter. I will not have the death of a valued client exploited and sensationalized by a private detective for his personal or professional profit."

"A worthy and wholesome attitude," Wolfe conceded. "I could remark that I would be hard put to make the affair more sensational than it already is, but even so your attitude is admirable. Only here's the rub: I'll tell you nothing whatever of the conversation I had yesterday with Mrs. Fromm."

"Then you're withholding evidence!"

"Pfui. I have reported it to the police. In writing, signed."

"Then why not to me?"

"Because I'm not a simpleton. I have reason to think that the conversation was one of the links in a chain that led to Mrs. Fromm's death, and if that is so, the person most eager to know what she said to me is probably her murderer."

"I'm not her murderer."

"That remains to be seen."

For a moment I thought Maddox was going to choke. His throat swelled visibly. But a veteran lawyer has had lots of practice controlling his reactions, and he managed it. "That's worse than stupidity, it's drivel."

"I disagree. Have the police talked with you?"

"Certainly."

"How many of them?"

"Two—no, three."

"Would you mind telling me who they were?"

"A Captain Bundy, and a sergeant, and Deputy Commissioner Youmans. Also Assistant District Attorney Mandelbaum."

"Did any of them tell you what Mrs. Fromm consulted me about yesterday?"

"No. We didn't get onto that."

"I suggest that you see someone at the District Attorney's office—preferably someone you know well—and ask him to tell you. If he does so, or if any other official does, without important reservations, I'll disgorge—your word—the money Mrs. Fromm paid me."

Maddox was looking as if someone were trying to persuade him that his nose was on upside down.

"I assure you," Wolfe went on, "that I am not ass enough to withhold evidence in a capital crime, especially not one as sensational as this. Indeed, I am meticulous about it. Unless the police have information about you that is unknown to me I doubt if they have hitherto regarded you as a likely suspect, but you may now find them a nuisance, after I have reported that you were so zealous to learn what Mrs. Fromm said to me that you went to all this trouble. That, of course, is my duty. This time it will also be my pleasure."

"You are—" He was about to choke again. "You are threatening to report this interview."

"Not a threat. Merely informing you that I will do so as soon as you leave."

"I'm leaving now." He was up. "I'll replevy that ten thousand dollars."

He wheeled and marched out. I followed to go and open the door for him, but he beat me to it, though he had to dive into the front room for his hat. When I returned to the office Horan was on his feet looking down at Wolfe, but no words were passing. Wolfe told me, "Get Mr. Cramer's office, Archie."

"Wait a minute." Horan's thin tenor was urgent. "You're making a mistake, Wolfe. If you really intend to investigate the murder. Investigate how? You had two of the persons closest to Mrs. Fromm and her affairs here in your office, and you have chased one of them out. Is that sensible?"

"Bosh." Wolfe was disgusted. "You won't even tell me whether Mrs. Fromm told you she came to me."

"The context of your question was offensive."

"Then I'll try being affable. Will you give me the substance of what was said at the gathering at your home last evening?"

Horan's long eyelashes fluttered. "I doubt if I should. Of course I have told the police all about it, and they have urged me to be discreet."

"Naturally. But will you?"

"No."

"Will you describe, fully and frankly, the nature and course of your relations with Mrs. Fromm?"

"Certainly not."

"If I send Mr. Goodwin to the office of the Association for the Aid of Displaced Persons, for which you are counsel, will you instruct the staff to answer his questions fully and freely?"

"No."

"So much for affability." Wolfe turned. "Get Mr. Cramer's office, Archie."

I swiveled and dialed WA 9-8241, and got a prompt response, but then it got complicated. None of our dear friends or enemies was available, and I finally had to settle for a Sergeant Griffin, and so informed Wolfe, who took his instrument and spoke.

"Mr. Griffin? Nero Wolfe speaking. This is for the information of Mr. Cramer, so please see that he gets it. Mr. James Albert Maddox and Mr. Dennis Horan, both attorneys-at-law, called on me this evening. You have the names correctly? Yes, I suppose they are familiar. They asked me to tell them about my conversation with Mrs. Damon Fromm when she came to my office yesterday. I refused, and they insisted. I won't go so far as to say that Mr. Maddox tried to bribe me, but I got the impression that if I told him about the conversation he wouldn't press me to return the money Mrs. Fromm paid me; otherwise, he would. Mr. Horan concurred, at least tacitly. When Mr. Maddox left in a huff, Mr. Horan told me I was making a mistake. Will you please see that this reaches Mr. Cramer? No, that's all now. If Mr. Cramer wants details or a signed statement I'll oblige him."

Wolfe hung up and muttered at the lawyer, "Are you still here?"

Horan was going, but in three steps he turned to say, "You may not know law, but you know how to skirt the edges of slander. After this performance I wonder how you got your reputation."

He went, and I got to the hall in time to see him emerge from the front room with his hat and depart. After chain-bolting the door, I went back to the office and observed enthusiastically, "Well, you certainly pumped them good! Milked 'em and stripped 'em. Congratulations!"

"Shut up," he told me, and picked up a book, not to throw.

9

I had been scheduled to leave Saturday afternoon for a weekend jaunt to Lily Rowan's fourteen-room shack in Westchester, but of course that had been knocked in the head—or rather, run over by a car. And my Sunday was no Sunday at all. Items:

Sergeant Purley Stebbins came bright and early, when

Wolfe was still up in his room with his breakfast tray, to get filled in on the invasion by the lawyers. I accommodated him. He was suspicious when he arrived, and more suspicious when he left. Though I explained that my employer was a genius and time would show that his stiff-arming them was a brilliant stroke, Purley refused to believe that Wolfe would have those two corralled in his office and not do his damndest to get a needle in. He did accept five or six crescents and two cups of coffee, but that was only because no man who has ever tasted Fritz's Sunday-morning crescents could possibly turn them down.

Wolfe and I both read every word of the accounts in the morning papers. Not that we hoped to get any hot leads, but at least we knew what the DA and Cramer had seen fit to release, and there were a few morsels to file for reference. Angela Wright, the Executive Secretary of Assadip, had formerly worked for Damon Fromm, and had been put in the Assadip job by him. Mrs. Fromm had supported more than forty charities and worthy causes, but Assadip had been her pet. Vincent Lipscomb, the publisher who had been at the dinner party at Horan's apartment, had run a series of articles on displaced persons in his magazine, *Modern Thought*, and was planning another. Mrs. Dennis Horan had formerly been a movie star—well, anyhow, she had acted in movies. Paul Kuffner handled public relations for Assadip as a public service without remuneration, but he had also been professionally engaged in the interest of Mrs. Fromm personally. Dennis Horan was an authority on international law, belonged to five clubs, and had a reputation as an amateur chef.

There still wasn't a word about the flap from Matthew Birch's pocket that had been retrieved from the chassis of the car that had killed Pete Drossos. The police were hanging onto that one. But because of the similarity of the manner of the killings, the Birch murder was getting a play too.

Wolfe phoned his lawyer, Henry Parker, to ask about the process of a replevin and to tell him to get set for one in case Maddox kept his promise to make a grab for the ten grand. I had to track Parker down at a country club on Long Island.

Not a peep out of Jean Estey.

During the day three reporters phoned, and two made

personal appearances on the stoop, but that was as far as they got. They didn't like it that the *Gazette* had had an exclusive on Nero Wolfe's working on the murder, and I sympathized with them.

My morning phone call to Lon Cohen at the *Gazette* was too early, and I left word for him to call me back, which he did. When I went there in the afternoon to collect a supply of prints of their best shots of the people we were interested in, I told Lon we could use a few dozen crucial inside facts, and he said he could too. He claimed they had printed everything they knew, though of course they had pecks of hot hearsay, such as that Mrs. Dennis Horan had once thrown a cocktail shaker at Mrs. Fromm, and that a certain importer had induced Vincent Lipscomb to publish an article favoring low tariffs by financing a trip to Europe. None of it seemed to me to be worth toting back to Thirty-fifth Street.

Anyway I had errands. For distribution of the photographs I met Saul Panzer at the Times Building, where he was boning up on displaced persons and Assadip; Orrie Cather at a bar and grill on Lexington Avenue, where he told me that the man who owed him a favor was playing golf at Van Cortlandt Park and could be seen later; and Fred Durkin at a restaurant on Broadway with his family, where Sunday dinner was $1.85 for adults and $1.15 for children. New York on a Sunday late in May is no place to open up a trail.

I made one little try on my own before heading back to Thirty-fifth Street. I don't remember ever doing a favor for a jewelry salesman, but I did a big one once for a certain member of the NYPD. If I had done my duty as a citizen and a licensed detective, he would have got it good and would still be locked up, but there were circumstances. No one knows about it, not even Wolfe. The man I did the favor for has given me to understand that he would like to hold my coat and hat if I ever get in a brawl, but as far as possible I've steered clear of him. That Sunday I thought what the hell, give the guy a chance to work it off, and I rang him and met him somewhere.

I said I would give him five minutes to tell me who had killed Mrs. Fromm. He said the way it was going it would take him five years and no guarantee. I asked him if that was based on the latest dispatches, and he said yes. I said that was all I wanted to know and therefore withdrew my offer of five minutes, but if and when he could make it five hours instead of five years I would appreciate it if he would communicate.

He asked, "Communicate what?"

I said, "That it's nearly ripe. That's all. So I can tell Mr. Wolfe to dive for cover."

"He's too damn fat to dive."

"I'm not."

"Okay, it's a deal. You sure that's all?"

"Absolutely."

"I thought maybe you were going to ask for Rowcliff's head with an apple in his mouth."

I went home and told Wolfe, "Relax. The cops are playing eeny, meeny, miney, mo. They know more than we do, but they're no closer to the answer."

"How do you know?"

"Gypsies. It's authentic, fresh, and strictly private. I saw the boys and gave them the photos. Do you want the unimportant details?"

"No."

"Any instructions?"

"No."

"No program for me for tomorrow?"

"No."

That was Sunday night.

Monday morning I got a treat. Wolfe never shows downstairs until eleven o'clock. After breakfast in his room he takes the elevator to the roof for the two hours with the plants before descending to the office. For morning communication with me he uses the house phone unless there is something special. Apparently that morning was special, for when Fritz came to the kitchen after taking breakfast up he announced solemnly, "Audience for you. *Levée!*" I spell it French because he pronounced it so.

I had finished with the morning paper, in which there was nothing to contradict my gypsies, and when my coffee cup was empty I ascended the one flight, knocked, and entered. On rainy mornings, or even gray ones, Wolfe breakfasts in bed, after tossing the black silk coverlet toward the foot because stains are bad for it, but when it's bright he has Fritz put the tray on a table near a window. That morning it was bright, and I had my treat. Barefooted, his hair tousled, with his couple of acres of yellow pajamas dazzling in the sun, he was sensational.

We exchanged good mornings, and he told me to sit. There was nothing left on his plate, but he wasn't through with the coffee.

"I have instructions," he informed me.

"Okay. I was intending to be at the bank at ten o'clock to deposit Mrs. Fromm's check."

"You may. You will proceed from there. You will probably be out all day. Tell Fritz to answer the phone and take the usual precautions with visitors. Report by phone at intervals."

"The funeral is at two o'clock."

"I know, and therefore you may come home for lunch. We'll see. Now the instructions."

He gave them to me. Four minutes did it. At the end he asked if I had any questions.

I was frowning. "One," I said. "It's clear enough as far as it goes, but what am I after?"

"Nothing."

"Then that's probably what I'll get."

He sipped coffee. "It's what I'll expect. You're stirring them up, that's all. You're turning a tiger loose in a crowd —or, if that's too bombastic, a mouse. How will they take it? Will any of them tell the police, and if so, which one or ones?"

I nodded. "Sure, I see the possibilities, but I wanted to know if there is any specific item I'm supposed to get."

"No. None." He reached for the coffee pot.

I went down to the office. In a drawer of my desk there is an assortment of calling cards, nine or ten different kinds, worded differently for different needs and occasions. I took some engraved ones with my name in the center and "Representing Nero Wolfe" in the corner, and on six of them I wrote in ink beneath my name, "To discuss what Mrs. Fromm told Mr. Wolfe on Friday." With them in my wallet, and the check and bankbook in my pocket, and a gun under my armpit, I was fully loaded, and I got my hat and beat it.

I walked to the bank, a pleasant fifteen-minute stretch

on a fine May morning, and from there took a taxi to Sixty-eighth Street. I didn't know what the home of a deceased millionairess would be like on the day of her funeral, which was to be held in a chapel on Madison Avenue, but outside it was quieter than it had been Saturday. The only evidences of anything uncommon were a cop in uniform on the sidewalk, with nothing to do, and black crepe hanging on the door. It wasn't the same cop as on Saturday, and this one recognized me. As I made for the door he stopped me.

"You want something?"

"Yes, officer, I do."

"You're Archie Goodwin. What do you want?"

"I want to ring that bell, and hand Peckham my card to take to Miss Estey, and enter, and be conducted within, and engage in conversation—"

"Yeah, you're Goodwin all right."

That called for no reply, and he merely stood, so I walked past him into the vestibule and pushed the bell. In a moment the door was opened by Peckham. He may have been well trained, but the sight of me was too much for him. Instead of keeping his eyes on my face, as any butler worthy of the name should do, he let his bewilderment show as he took in my brown tropical worsted, light tan striped shirt, brown tie, and tan shoes. In fairness to him, remember it was the day of the funeral.

I handed him a card. "Miss Estey, please?"

He admitted me, but he had an expression on his face. He probably thought I was batty, since from the facts as he knew them that was the simplest explanation. Instead of ushering me down the hall, he told me to wait there, and went to the door to the office and disappeared inside. Voices issued, too low for me to catch the words, and then he came out.

"This way, Mr. Goodwin."

He moved aside as I approached, and I passed through the door. Jean Estey was there at a desk with my card in her hand. Without bothering with any greeting, she asked me abruptly, "Will you please close the door?"

I did so and turned to her. She spoke. "You know what I told you Saturday, Mr. Goodwin."

The greenish-brown eyes were straight at me. Below

them the skin was puffy, either from too little sleep or too much, and while I still would have called her comely, she looked as if the two days since I had seen her had been two years.

I went to a chair near the end of her desk and sat. "You mean about the police asking you to see Nero Wolfe and pass it on?"

"Yes."

"What about it?"

"Nothing, only—well—if Mr. Wolfe still wants to see me, I think I might go. I'm not sure—but I certainly wouldn't tell the police what he said. I think they're simply awful. It's been more than two days since Mrs. Fromm was killed, fifty-nine hours, and I don't think they're getting anywhere at all."

I had to make a decision in about one second. With the line she was taking, it was a cinch I could get her down to the office, but would Wolfe want her? Which would he want me to do, get her to the office or follow my instructions? I don't know what I would have decided if I could have gone into a huddle with myself to think it over, but it had to be a flash vote and it went for instructions.

I spoke. "I'll tell Mr. Wolfe how you feel, Miss Estey, and I'm sure he'll be glad to hear it, but I ought to explain that what it says on that card—'Representing Nero Wolfe' —is not exactly true. I'm here on my own."

She cocked her head. "On your own? Don't you work for Nero Wolfe?"

"Sure I do, but I work for me too when I get a good chance. I have an offer to make you."

She glanced at the card. "It says 'To discuss what Mrs. Fromm told Mr. Wolfe on Friday.'"

"That's right, that's what I want to discuss, but just between you and me."

"I don't understand."

"You soon will." I leaned toward her and lowered my voice. "You see, I was present during the talk Mrs. Fromm had with Mr. Wolfe. All of it. I have an extremely good memory. I could recite it to you word for word, or mighty close to it."

"Well?"

"Well, I think you would appreciate hearing it. I have

reason to believe you would find it very interesting. You may think I'm sticking my neck out, but I have been Mr. Wolfe's confidential assistant for a good many years, and I've done some good work for him, and I've seen to it that he has learned to trust me, and if you call him up when I leave here, or go to see him, and tell him what I said to you, he'll think you're trying to pull a fast one. And when he asks me and I tell him you're a dirty liar, he'll believe me. So don't worry about my neck. I'll tell you about that talk, all of it, for five thousand dollars cash."

She said, "Oh," or maybe it was "Uh," but it was just a noise. Then she just stared.

"Naturally," I said, "I don't expect you to have that amount in your purse, so this afternoon will do, but I'll have to be paid in advance."

"This is incredible," she said. "Why on earth should I pay you five cents to tell me about that talk? Let alone five thousand dollars. Why?"

I shook my head. "That would be telling. After you pay and I deliver, you may or may not feel that you got your money's worth. I'm giving no guarantee of satisfaction, but I'd be a fool to come here with such an offer if all I had was a bag of popcorn."

Her gaze left me. She opened a drawer to get a pack of cigarettes, removed one, tapped its end several times on a memo pad, and reached for a desk lighter. But the cigarette didn't get lit. She dropped it and put the lighter down. "I suppose," she said, her eyes back to me, "I should be insulted and indignant, and I suppose I will, but now I'm too shocked. I didn't know you were a common skunk. If I had that much money to toss around I'd like to pay you and hear it. I'd like to hear what kind of a lie you're trying to sell me. You'd better go." She rose. "Get out of here!"

"Miss Estey, I think—"

"Get out!"

I have seen skunks in motion, both skunks unperturbed and skunks in a hurry, and they are not dignified. I was. Taking my hat from a corner of the desk, I walked out. In the hall Peckham showed his relief at getting rid of a lunatic undertaker without regrettable incident by bowing to me as he held the door open. On the sidewalk the cop thought he would say something and then decided no.

Around the corner I found a phone booth in a drugstore, called Wolfe and gave him a full report as instructed, and flagged a taxi headed downtown.

The address of my second customer, on Gramercy Park, proved to be an old yellow brick apartment house with a uniformed doorman, a spacious lobby with fine old rugs, and an elevator with a bad attack of asthma. It finally got the chauffeur and me to the eighth floor, after the doorman had phoned up and passed me. When I pushed the button at the door of 8B it was opened by a female master sergeant dressed like a maid, who admitted me, took my hat, and directed me to an archway at the end of the hall.

It was a large high-ceilinged living room, more than fully furnished, the dominant colors of its drapes and upholstery and rugs being yellow, violet, light green, and maroon—at least that was the impression gained from a glance around. A touch of black was supplied by the dress of the woman who moved to meet me as I approached. The black was becoming to her, with her ash-blond hair gathered into a bun at the back, her clear blue eyes, and her pale carefully tended skin. She didn't offer a hand, but her expression was not hostile.

"Mrs. Horan?" I inquired.

She nodded. "My husband will be furious at me for seeing you, but I was simply too curious. Of course I should be sure—you are the Archie Goodwin that works for Nero Wolfe?"

I got a card from my wallet and handed it to her, and she held it at an angle for better light. Then she widened her eyes at me. "But I don't—'To discuss what Mrs. Fromm told Mr. Wolfe'? With me? Why with me?"

"Because you're Mrs. Dennis Horan."

"Yes, I am, of course." Her tone implied that that angle hadn't occurred to her. "My husband will be furious!"

I glanced over my shoulder. "Perhaps we might sit over by a window? This is rather private."

"Certainly." She turned and found a way among pieces of furniture, and I followed. She took a chair at the far end near a window, and I moved one over close enough to make it cozy.

"You know," she said, "this is the most dreadful thing. The most dreadful. Laura Fromm was such a fine person."

She might have used the same tone and expression to tell
me she liked the way I had my hair cut. She added, "Did
you know her well?"

"No, I saw her only once, last Friday when she came to
consult Mr. Wolfe."

"He's a detective, isn't he?"

"That's right."

"Are you a detective too?"

"Yes, I work for Mr. Wolfe."

"It's simply fascinating. Of course there have been two
men here asking questions—no, three—and Saturday more
of them at the District Attorney's office, but they're really
only policemen. You're truly a detective. I would never
have thought a detective would be so—would dress so
well." She made a pretty little gesture. "But here I am
babbling along as usual, and you want to discuss something
with me, don't you?"

"That was the idea. What Mrs. Fromm said to Mr.
Wolfe."

"Then you'll have to tell me what she said. I can't discuss it until I know what it was. Can I?"

"No," I conceded, "but I can't tell you until I know
how much you want to hear it."

"Oh, I do want to hear it!"

"Good. I thought you would. You see, Mrs. Horan, I
was in the room all the time Mrs. Fromm and Mr. Wolfe
were talking, and I remember every word they said. That's
why I thought you would be extremely curious about it, so
I'm not surprised that you are. The trouble is, I can't
afford to satisfy your curiosity as a gift. I should have explained, I'm not here representing Nero Wolfe, that's why
I said it's rather private. I'm representing just myself. I'll
satisfy your curiosity if you'll lend me five thousand dollars
to be repaid the day it rains up instead of down."

The only visible reaction was that the blue eyes widened
a little. "That's an amusing idea," she said, "raining up instead of down. Would it be raining from the clouds up, or
up from the ground to the clouds?"

"Either way would do."

"I like it better up from the ground." A pause. "What
did you say about lending you some money? I beg your
pardon, but my mind got onto the raining up."

I was ready to admit she was too much for me, but I struggled on. I abandoned the rain. "If you'll pay me five thousand dollars I'll tell you what Mrs. Fromm told Mr. Wolfe. Cash in advance."

Her eyes widened. "Was that what you said? I guess I didn't understand."

"I made it fancy by dragging in the rain. Sorry. It's better that way, plain."

She shook her pretty head. "It's not better for me, Mr. Goodwin. It sounds absolutely crazy, unless—oh, I see! You mean she told him something awful about me! That doesn't surprise me any, but what was it?"

"I didn't say she said anything about you. I merely—"

"But of course she did! She would! What was it?"

"No." I was emphatic. "Maybe I didn't make it plain enough." I stuck up a finger. "First you give me money." Another finger. "Second, I give you facts. I'm offering to sell you something, that's all."

She nodded regretfully. "That's the real trouble."

"What is?"

"Why, you don't really mean it. If you offered to tell me for twenty dollars that might be different, and of course I'd love to know what she said—but five thousand! Do you know what I think, Mr. Goodwin?"

"I do not."

"I think you're much too fine a person to use this kind of tactics to stir up my curiosity just to get me talking. When you walked in I wouldn't have dreamed you were like that, especially your eyes. I go by eyes."

I also go by eyes up to a point, and hers didn't fit her performance. Though not the keenest and smartest I had ever seen, they were not the eyes of a scatterbrain. I would have liked to stay an hour or so to make a stab at tagging her, but my instructions were to put it bluntly, note the reaction, and move on; and besides, I wanted to get in as many as possible before funeral time. So I arose to leave. She was sorry to see me go; she even hinted that she might add ten to her counteroffer of twenty bucks; but I let her know that her remark about my tactics had hurt my feelings and I wanted to be alone.

Down on the street I found a phone booth to report to Wolfe and then took a taxi to Forty-second Street.

I had been informed by Lon Cohen that I shouldn't
mark it against the Association for the Aid of Displaced
Persons that they sported an elegant sunny office on the
twenty-sixth floor of one of the newer midtown commer-
cial palaces, because Mrs. Fromm owned the building and
they paid no rent. Even so, it was a lot of dog for an outfit
devoted to the relief of the unfortunate and oppressed.
There in the glistening reception room I had an example
before my eyes. At one end of a brown leather settee,
slumped in weariness and despair, wearing an old gray suit
two sizes too large for him, was a typical specimen. As I
shot him a glance I wondered how it impressed him, but
then I glanced again and quit wondering. It was Saul
Panzer. Our eyes met, then his fell, and I went to the
woman at the desk, who had a long thin nose and a chin
to match.

She said Miss Wright was engaged and was available
only for appointments. After producing a card and per-
suading her to relay not only my name but the message
under it, I was told I would be received, but she didn't like
it. She made it clear, with her tight lips and the set of her
jaw, that she wanted no part of me.

I was shown into a large corner room with windows on
two sides, giving views of Manhattan south and east. There
were two desks, but only one of them was occupied, by a
brown-haired female executive who looked almost as weary
as Saul Panzer but wasn't giving in to it and didn't intend to.

She greeted me with a demand. "May I see your card,
please?"

It had been read to her on the phone. I crossed and
handed it over. She looked at it and then up at me. "I'm
very busy. Is this urgent?"

"It won't take long, Miss Wright."

"What good will it do to discuss it with me?"

"I don't know. You'll have to leave that open, whether
it does any good or not. I'm speaking strictly for myself,
not for Nero Wolfe, and there's no—"

"Didn't Nero Wolfe send you here?"

"No."

"Did the police?"

"No. This is my idea. I've had some bad luck and I need

some cash, and I've got something to sell. I know this is a bad day for you, with Mrs. Fromm's funeral this afternoon, but this won't keep—at least I can't count on it—and I need five thousand dollars as soon as I can get it."

She smiled with one side of her mouth. "I'm afraid I haven't that much with me, if this is a stickup. Aren't you a reputable licensed detective?"

"I try to be. As I said, I've had some bad luck. All I'm doing, I'm offering to sell you something, and you can take it or leave it. It depends on how much you would like to know exactly what Mrs. Fromm told Mr. Wolfe. At five thousand dollars it might be a swell bargain for you, or it might not. You would be a better judge of that than I am, but of course you can't know until after you hear it."

She regarded me. "So that's it," she said.

"That's it," I concurred.

Her brown eyes were harder to meet than Jean Estey's had been, or Claire Horan's. My problem was to have the look of a man with a broad streak of rat in him, but also one who could be depended on to deliver as specified. Her straight hard gaze gave me a feeling that I wasn't dressed right for the part, and I was trying to give orders to my face not to show it. The face felt as if it might help to be doing something, so I used my mouth. "You understand, Miss Wright, this is a bona fide offer. I can and will tell you everything they said."

"But you would want the money first." Her voice was as hard as her eyes.

I turned a hand over. "I'm afraid that's the only way we could do it. You could tell me to go soak my head."

"So I could." Her mind was working. "Perhaps we can arrange a compromise." She got a pad of paper from a drawer and pushed her desk pen across. "Pull up a chair, or use the other desk, and put your offer in writing, briefly. Put it like this: 'Upon payment to me by Angela Wright of five thousand dollars in cash, I will relate to her, in full and promptly, the conversation that took place between Laura Fromm and Nero Wolfe last Friday afternoon.' And date it and sign it, that's all."

"And give it to you?"

"Yes. I'll return it as soon as you have kept your side of the bargain. Isn't that fair?"

I smiled down at her. "Now really, Miss Wright. If I were as big a sap as that how long do you think I would have lasted with Nero Wolfe?"

She smiled back. "Would you like to know what I think?"

"Sure."

"I think that if you were capable of selling secrets you learned in Wolfe's office he would have known it long ago and would have thrown you out."

"I said I had some bad luck."

"Not that bad. I'm not a sap either. Of course you're right about one thing—that is, Mr. Wolfe is—I would like very much to know what Mrs. Fromm consulted him about. Naturally. I wonder what would actually happen if I scraped up the money and handed it over?"

"There's an easy way of finding out."

"Perhaps there's an easier one. I could go to Mr. Wolfe and ask him."

"I'd call you a liar."

She nodded. "Yes, I suppose you would. He couldn't very well admit he had sent you with such an offer."

"Especially if he didn't."

The brown eyes flashed for an instant and then were hard again. "Do you know what I resent most, Mr. Goodwin? I resent being taken for a complete fool. That's my vanity. Tell Mr. Wolfe that. Tell him that I don't mind his trying this little trick on me, but I do mind his underrating me."

I grinned at her. "You like that idea, don't you?"

"Yes, it appeals to me strongly."

"Okay, hang onto it. For that there's no charge."

I turned and went. As I passed through the reception room and saw Saul there on the settee I would have liked to warn him that he was up against a mind-reader, but of course had to skip it.

Down in the lobby I found a phone booth and reported to Wolfe and then went to a fountain for a Coke, partly because I was thirsty and partly because I wanted time out for a post-mortem. Had I bungled it, or was she too damn smart for me, or what? As I finished the Coke I decided that the only way to keep feminine intuition from sneaking through an occasional lucky stab was to stay away from women altogether, which wasn't practical. Anyhow, Wolfe hadn't seemed to think it mattered, since I had made her the offer and that was the chief point.

It was a short walk to my next stop, an older and dingier office building on Forty-third Street west of Fifth Avenue. After taking the elevator to the fourth floor and entering a door that was labeled *Modern Thoughts*, I got a pleasant surprise. Having on Sunday bought a copy of the magazine that Vincent Lipscomb edited, and looked through it before passing it to Wolfe, I had supposed that any female employed by it would have all her points of interest, if any, inside her skull; but a curvy little number with dancing eyes, seated at a switchboard, gave me one bright glance and then welcomed me with a smile which indicated that the only reason she had taken the job was that she thought I would show up someday.

I would have enjoyed cooperating by asking her what kind of orchids she liked, but it would soon be noon, so I merely returned the smile, told her I wanted to see Mr. Lipscomb, and handed her a card.

"A card?" she said appreciatively. "Real style, huh?" Seeing what was on it, she gave me a second look, still friendly but more reserved, inserted a plug with lively fingers, pressed a button, and in a moment spoke into the transmitter.

She pulled out the plug, handed me the card, and said, "Through there and third door on the left."

I didn't have to count to three because as I started down the dark narrow hall a door opened and a man appeared and bellowed at me as if I had been across a river, "In here!" Then he went back in. When I entered he was standing with his back to a window with his hands thrust into his pants pockets. The room was small, and the one desk and two chairs could have been picked up on Second Avenue for the price of a pair of Warburton shoes.

"Mr. Lipscomb?"

"Yes."

"You know who I am."

"Yes."

His voice, though below a bellow, was up to five times as many decibels as were needed. It could have been to match his stature, for he was two inches above me, with massive shoulders that much wider; or it could have been in compensation for his nose, which was wide and flat and would have spoiled any map no matter what the rest of it was.

"This is a confidential matter," I told him. "Personal and private."

"Yes."

"And between you and me only. My proposition is just from me and it's just for you."

"What is it?"

"An offer to exchange information for cash. Since you're a magazine editor, that's an old story to you. For five thousand dollars I'll tell you about the talk Mrs. Fromm had with Mr. Wolfe last Friday. Authentic and complete."

He removed a hand from a pocket to scratch a cheek, then put it back. When he spoke his voice was down to a reasonable level. "My dear fellow, I'm not Harry Luce. Anyway, magazines don't buy like that. The procedure is this: you tell me in confidence what you have, and then, if I can use it, we agree on the amount. If we can't agree, no one is out anything." He raised the broad shoulders and let them drop. "I don't know. I shall certainly run a piece on Laura Fromm, a thoughtful and provocative piece; she was a great woman and a great lady; but at the moment I don't see how your information would fit in. What's it like?"

"I don't mean for your magazine, Mr. Lipscomb, I mean for your personally."

He frowned. If he wasn't straight he was good. "I'm afraid I don't get you."

"It's perfectly simple. I heard that talk, all of it. That evening Mrs. Fromm was murdered, and you're involved, and I have—"

"That's absurd. I am not involved. Words are my specialty, Mr. Goodwin, and one difficulty with them is that everybody uses them, too often in ignorance of their proper meaning. I'm willing to assume that you used that word in ignorance—otherwise it was slanderous. I am not involved."

"Okay. Are you concerned?"

"Of course I am. I wasn't intimate with Mrs. Fromm, but I esteemed her highly and was proud to know her."

"You were at the party at Horan's Friday evening. You were one of the last to see her alive. The police, who specialize in words too in a way, have asked you a lot of questions and will ask you more. But say you're concerned. Everything considered, including what I heard Mrs. Fromm tell Mrs. Wolfe, I thought you might be concerned five thousand dollars' worth."

"This begins to sound like blackmail. Is it?"

"Search me. You're the word specialist. I'm ignorant."

His hands abruptly left his pockets, and for a second I thought he was going to make contact, but he only rubbed his palms together. "If it's blackmail," he said, "there must be a threat. If I pay, what then?"

"No threat. You get the information, that's all."

"And if I don't pay?"

"You don't get it."

"Who does?"

I shook my head. "I said no threat. I'm just trying to sell you something."

"Of course. A threat doesn't have to be explicit. It has been published that Wolfe is investigating the death of Mrs. Fromm."

"Right."

"But she didn't engage him to do that, since surely she wasn't anticipating her death. This is how it looks. She paid Wolfe to investigate something or somebody, and that evening she was killed. He considered himself under obligation to investigate her death. You can't be offering to sell me information that Wolfe regards as being connected with her death, because you couldn't possibly suppress such evidence without Wolfe's connivance, and you're not claiming that, are you?"

"No."

"Then what you're offering is information, something Mrs. Fromm told Wolfe, that need not be disclosed as related to her death. Isn't that correct?"

"No comment."

He shook his head. "That won't do. Unless you tell me that, I couldn't possibly deal with you. I don't say I will deal if you do tell me, but without that I can't decide."

He about-faced and was looking out the window, if his eyes were open. All I had was his broad back. He stayed that way long enough to take his temperature, and then some. Finally he turned.

"I don't see that it would help any, Goodwin, for me to characterize your conduct as it deserves. Good God, what a way to make a living! Here I am, giving all my time and talent and energy in an effort to improve the tone of human conduct—and there you are. But that doesn't interest you—all you care about is money. Good God! Money! I'll think it over. I may phone you and I may not. You're in the book?"

I told him yes, Nero Wolfe's number, and, not caring to hear any more ugly facts about myself as compared to him, I slunk out. My cheerful little friend at the switchboard might have been willing to buck me up some, but I felt it would be bad for her to have any contact with my kind of character and went right on by.

Down the street I found a phone booth, dialed the number I knew best, and had Wolfe's voice in my ear.

"Ready with Number Four," I told him. "Lipscomb. Are you comfortable?"

"Go ahead. No questions."

His saying "No questions" meant that he was not alone. So I took extra care to give it all to him, including my spot opinion of the improver of the tone of human conduct. That done, I told him it was twenty minutes past twelve, to save him the trouble of looking up at the clock, and asked if I should proceed to Number Five, Paul Kuffner, the public-relations adviser who had operated on me so smoothly when he found me with Jean Estey.

"No," he said curtly. "Come home at once. Mr. Paul Kuffner is here, and I want to see you."

10 The tone and wording of Wolfe's command had of course warned me what to expect, so I wasn't surprised at the dirty look he gave me as I entered the office. Paul Kuffner, in the red leather chair, didn't turn on the smile of enthusiastic approval he had favored me with Saturday, but I wouldn't have called his expression hostile. I suppose sound public relations rule out open hostility to a fellow being unless he actually chews on your ear. One little bite wouldn't be enough.

As I sat at my desk Wolfe spoke. "Don't sit there, Archie. Your right to sit at that desk is suspended." He pointed to one of the yellow chairs. "Move, please."

I was astounded. "What! What's the idea?"

"Move, please." He was grim.

I told my face that in addition to being astounded I was hurt and bewildered, as I arose, went to the yellow chair, lowered myself, and met his withering gaze. His tone matched. "Mr. Kuffner has made a shocking accusation. I want you to hear it from him. Mr. Kuffner?"

It pained Kuffner to have to say it. His thick wide mouth puckered, making an arc of his plucked-eyebrow mustache. He addressed me, not Wolfe. "I am informed that you made an offer this morning to a woman whose veracity I rely upon. She says that you offered to tell her all about the talk Mrs. Fromm had with Mr. Wolfe last Friday, if she would first pay you five thousand dollars in cash."

I did not leap from my chair in indignation. Being a veteran detective of wide experience under the guidance of Nero Wolfe, I should be able to meet a contemptible frame-up with some poise. I raised my chin a quarter of an inch and asked him, "What's the woman's name?"

He shook his head. "I haven't told Mr. Wolfe because she requested me not to. Of course you know it."

"I've forgotten. Tell me."

"No."

"For God's sake." I was mildly disgusted. "If you were a United States Senator, naturally I wouldn't expect you to name my accuser, but since you're not, go climb a tree."

Kuffner was distressed but stubborn. "It seems to me quite simple. All I ask you to do is answer the question, did you make such an offer to any woman this morning?"

"Okay, say I answer it. Then you say that some man told you that I stole the cheese out of his mousetrap last night, and did I, and I answer that. Then you say that some horse told you that I cut off his tail—"

"That will do," Wolfe put in. "He does have a point,

Mr. Kuffner. Anonymous accusations are in questionable taste."

"It's not anonymous to me. I know her."

"Then name her."

"I was asked not to."

"If you promised not to I'm afraid we're at an impasse. I'm not surprised that Mr. Goodwin makes this demand; he would be a ninny if he didn't. So that ends it. I shall not pursue it. If you are not justified in expecting an answer to an anonymous accusation, neither am I."

Kuffner puckered his mouth, and the mustache was a parenthesis lying on its back. His hand went automatically to his side pocket and came out with a cigarette case. He opened it and removed one, looked at it and became aware of it, and asked, "May I smoke?"

"No," Wolfe said flatly,

That was by no means a hard and fast rule. It had been relaxed not only for some men, but even for a few women, not necessarily prospective clients. Kuffner was frustrated and confused. A performance of a basic habit had been arbitrarily stopped, and also he had a problem. Taking a cigarette from a metal case with a clamp needs only a flick of a finger and thumb, but putting one back in is more complicated. He solved it by returning the case to his left side pocket and putting the cigarette in his right one. He was trying not to be flustered, but his voice showed it. "It was Miss Angela Wright."

I met it like a man. "Miss Wright told you that?"

"Yes."

"That I made her that offer?"

"Yes."

I got up and made for my desk. Wolfe asked, "What are you doing?"

"Phoning Miss Wright to ask her. If she says yes, I'll call her a purebred liar and offer her a pedigree certificate for five thousand bucks."

"She's not there," Kuffner said.

"Where is she?"

"She was going to get a bite of lunch and then go to the chapel where the funeral will be held."

"Did you," Wolfe asked, "make Miss Wright an offer as described by Mr. Kuffner?"

"No, sir."

"Did you say anything to her that could have been reasonably construed as such an offer?"

"No, sir."

"Did anyone else hear your conversation with her?"

"Not unless that room is wired for sound."

"Then sit at your desk, please." Wolfe turned to the visitor. "If you have correctly reported what Miss Wright told you, it is an issue of veracity between her and Mr. Goodwin. I believe Mr. Goodwin. Other than what you have said, have you any evidence to impeach him?"

"No evidence, no."

"Do you still believe Miss Wright?"

"I—yes. I do."

"Then there we are. You realize, I suppose, that for me it is not exclusively a choice between Miss Wright and Mr. Goodwin as the liar, since I have no knowledge of what she told you except your own statement."

Kuffner smiled. He had caught up now and was bland again. "We might as well make it unanimous, Mr. Wolfe. I didn't mention this because it was only an inference by Miss Wright. It is her opinion that you sent Goodwin to her to make that offer. So for me too they are not the only alternatives."

Wolfe nodded, unconcerned. "Once the fabric is woven it may be embellished at will." He glanced at the clock. "It's twenty minutes to my lunchtime. We're at a dead end and might as well quit unless you want to proceed on a hypothesis. We can assume that either Miss Wright or you is lying, or we can assume that Mr. Goodwin is, or he and I both are. I'm quite willing, as a basis for discussion, to assume the last. That's the best position you could possibly have expected to occupy. What then?"

Kuffner was ready for it. "Then I ask you how you can justify making an improper and coercive proposal to Miss Wright."

"I reply that you have no mandate to regulate my conduct. Then?"

"I would decide—this would be with reluctance—I would probably decide that it was my duty to inform the police that you were interfering with official investigation of a murder."

"Nonsense. My talk with Mrs. Fromm has been reported to them, but not with a copyright. I'm not an attorney, and what a client says to me is not privileged. There was no interference or impropriety, and certainly no coercion. I had something that was legally and rightfully in my possession, a record of a talk, and I offered to sell it, with no attempt at compulsion of any hint of a disagreeable alternative. Your decision to report it to the police doesn't interest me."

Kuffner was smiling. "You certainly were prepared for that."

"I should have been. I framed the hypothesis. What next?"

The smile disappeared. "I would like to drop the hypothesis. Even if I could prove the offer was made—and I can't, except for Miss Wright's word—since you think you can justify it—and I'll grant you're right for the sake of argument—where would that get me? We haven't much time left—I must get to the funeral—and I want to get down to business."

"Your business or mine?"

"Both." Kuffner leaned forward. "My professional function, Mr. Wolfe, is to give advice to my clients, and to some extent handle their affairs, so that they and their activities will be regarded in a favorable light. Mrs. Fromm was one of my clients. Another was, and is, the Association for the Aid of Displaced Persons. I have a strong feeling of obligation to Mrs. Fromm which was not diminished by her death—on the contrary, I will do anything in my power to see that her memory and reputation are not damaged. Also I am concerned about the Association. As far as I know, there was no connection between her death and the Association's affairs, but it is possible that there was one. Do you know of any?"

"Go on, Mr. Kuffner."

"I am. I think it is more than possible, it is very probable, that there was a connection between Mrs. Fromm's death and her talk with you on Friday. What she consulted you about must have been secret, because to my knowledge she told no one of coming to see you. It would have been the natural thing for her to tell me, that's obvious, but she didn't. It must have been important, because she certainly wouldn't have called on a private detective, especially you, about anything trivial. And if it was connected with whatever and whoever killed her, it must have been more than important, it must have been vital. I want to know about it—I *need* to know about it. I have tried to get the police to tell me—and they won't. You have just said that the record of that talk is legally and rightfully in your possession and it wouldn't be improper for you to sell it. I'll pay you five thousand dollars for it. Cash in advance. If you want it in currency I can have it this afternoon."

Wolfe was frowning at him. "Which is it, Mr. Kuffner, black or white? You can't have it both ways. You were going to report an iniquitous proposal to the police, and now you are ready to be a party to it. An extraordinary ethical somersault."

"No more extraordinary than yours," Kuffner contended. "You were condemning Goodwin for it—you even ordered him away from his desk—and then you justified it."

"Certainly. Mr. Goodwin would have been offering to sell something that doesn't belong to him; it belongs to me." Wolfe flipped a hand. "But your dexterity as a casuistic acrobat, though impressive, is collateral. The question is, do I accept your offer? The answer is no. I must decline it."

Kuffner's fist hit the chair arm. "You can't decline! You can't!"

"No?"

"No! I have a right to demand this as the representative of Mrs. Fromm's interests! You have no right to decline! It's improper interference with my legitimate function!"

Wolfe shook his head. "If there were no other reason for my refusal it would be enough that I'm afraid to deal with you. You're much too agile for me. Only minutes ago it was improper interference for me to offer to sell the information; now it's improper interference for me to refuse to sell it. You have me befuddled, and I must at least have time to get my bearings. I know how to reach you." He glanced at the clock. "You'll be late for the funeral."

That was true. Kuffner glanced at his wrist and arose. He was obviously, from his face, deciding that he must depart in a favorable light. He smiled at me and then at Wolfe.

"I apologize," he said, "for being too free with my accusations. I hope you'll make allowances. This is by far the worst situation I've ever had to deal with. By far. I'll be expecting and hoping to hear from you."

By the time I got back from showing him out Wolfe had crossed the hall to the dining room.

11   At six-thirty that afternoon I sat on a hard wooden chair in the office of Assistant District Attorney Mandelbaum, a smallish room, making a speech.

The audience of three was big enough for the room. At his desk was Mandelbaum, middle-aged, plump, to be classified as bald in two years. At his elbow was a Homicide dick named Randall, tall and narrow, with nothing covering his bones but his skin at the high spots. Jean Estey, in a chair near the end of the desk, around the corner from me, was in a dark gray dress which didn't go too well with her greenish-brown eyes, but presumably it was the best she had had in stock for the funeral.

The conference, consisting mostly of questions by Mandelbaum and answers by Miss Estey and me, had gone on for ten minutes or so when I felt that the background had been laid for my speech, and I proceeded to make it.

"I don't blame you," I told Mandelbaum, "for wasting your time, or even mine, because I know that nine-tenths of a murder investigation is barking up empty trees, but hasn't this gone on long enough? Where are we? No matter what the facts are, I bow out. If Miss Estey made it all up, you don't need me to help you try to find out why. If she's telling the truth and I made her that offer on my own, you told Mr. Wolfe about it on the phone, and he's the one to put me through the wringer, not you. If Wolfe sent me to make her the offer, as you prefer to believe, what's all the racket about? He could put an ad in the paper offering to sell a transcript of his talk with Mrs. Fromm to anyone who would pay the price, which might not be very noble and you wouldn't like it, but what would the charge read like? I came down here at your request, and now I'd like to go home and try to convince my employer that I'm not a viper in his bosom."

It wasn't quite that easy, but after another five minutes I was allowed to depart without shooting my way out. Jean Estey didn't offer to kiss me good-by.

I really did want to get home, because I would have to eat dinner early in order to keep a date with Orrie Cather. Around five o'clock he had showed up at the office with a report that seemed to justify annoying Wolfe in the plant rooms, and I had taken him up. Wolfe was grumpy but he listened. The salesman at Boudet's had never seen spider earrings, gold or otherwise, but he had given Orrie a list of names of people connected with manufacturers, importers, wholesalers, and retailers, and Orrie had gone after them, mostly by phone. By four o'clock he had been about ready to report that there had never been a spider earring in New York, when a buyer for a wholesaler suggested that he speak to Miss Grummon, the firm's shopper.

Miss Grummon said yes, she had seen one pair of spider earrings, and she didn't care to see more. One day a few weeks ago—she couldn't give the exact date—walking along Forty-sixth Street, she had stopped to inspect a window display and there they were, two big golden spiders in a green-lined case. She had thought them horrid, certainly not a design to suggest to her employers, and had been surprised to see them displayed by Julius Gerster, since most of the items offered in his small shop showed excellent taste.

So far fine. But Orrie had made straight for Gerster's shop and had stubbed his toe. He claimed he had made a good approach, telling Gerster he had seen the earrings in the window and wanted to buy them, but Gerster had clammed up from the beginning. He didn't deny that there had once been a pair of spider earrings in his shop, but neither did he admit it. His position, stated in the fewest possible words, was that he had no recollection of such an item, and if he had displayed it he didn't remember how or to whom they had been disposed of. Orrie's position, stated to Wolfe and me in enough words, was that Gerster was a goddam liar and that he wanted permission to pour gasoline on him and light him.

So Orrie and I were to call on Mr. Gerster at his home that evening, not by appointment.

During the day there had been various other occurrences not worth detailing—calls from Saul Panzer and Fred Durkin, who had found nothing to bring in, and nudges from Lon Cohen. One non-occurrence should be mentioned: there had been no word of a replevin by James Albert Maddox. Our lawyer, Parker, was feeling slighted.

I met Orrie at eight o'clock at the corner of Seventy-fourth and Columbus, and we walked east to the number, nearly to Central Park West, through a monotonous drizzle that had started in late afternoon. If New York apartment houses can be divided into two classes, those with canopies and those without, this one was in between. The stanchions were there, from the entrance to the curb, but there was no covering canvas. In the lobby we told the doorman "Gerster," and kept going to the elevator. The elevator man said it was 11F.

The door was opened by an eighth-grader about the age and build of Pete Drossos, but very neat and clean. The instant I saw him I ditched the strategy we had decided on and elected another. I said to Orrie, "Thanks for bringing me up. See you later." It took him about a second to get it, which wasn't bad. He said, "Don't mention it," and headed for the elevator. The boy had told me good evening, and I returned it, gave him my name, and said I wanted to see Mr. Julius Gerster. He said, "I'll tell him, sir. Please wait," and disappeared. I didn't cross the sill. Soon a man came, clear up to me before speaking. He was some shorter than me, and older, with a small tidy face and black hair brushed back smooth, fully as neat and clean as his son—at least I hoped it was his son.

He asked politely but coolly, "You wanted to see me?"

"I would like to if it's convenient. My name's Goodwin, and I work for Nero Wolfe, the detective. I want to ask you something about the murder of a boy—a twelve-year-old boy named Peter Drossos."

His expression didn't change. As I was to see, it never

changed. "I know nothing about the murder of any boy," he declared.

I contradicted him. "Yes, you do, but you don't know you do. What you know may be essential to the discovery of the boy's murderer. Mr. Wolfe thinks it is. May I come in for five minutes and explain?"

"Are you a policeman?"

"No, sir. Private detective. The boy was willfully run over by a car. It was a brutal murder."

He stepped aside. "Come in."

He took me not to the front, from where he had come, but along the hall in the other direction, into a small room with all its walls covered with books and pictures. There were a little desk in a corner, a chess table by a window, and two upholstered chairs. He motioned me to one, and, when I was seated, took the other.

I told him about Pete, not at great length, but enough for him to get the picture complete—his session with Wolfe and me, his second visit the next day only a few hours before Stebbins came with the news of his death, and Mrs. Drossos's call to bring the message and the four dollars and thirty cents. I didn't ham it, I just told it. Then I went after him.

"There are complications," I said, "that I won't go into unless you want them. For instance, Mrs. Damon Fromm was wearing gold spiders for earrings when she was killed Friday night. But what I'm asking your help on is who killed the boy. The police have got nowhere. Neither has Mr. Wolfe. In his opinion the best chance to start a trail is the earrings that Pete said the woman in the car was wearing. We can't find anyone who has ever seen any woman with such earrings—except Mrs. Fromm, of course—and Mr. Wolfe decided to try starting at the other end. He put a man on it, a man named Cather, to dig up someone who had ever sold spider earrings. By this afternoon Cather was about ready to decide there was no such person or firm in New York, and then he hit it. A reliable person, who can be produced if necessary, told him that she saw a pair in the window of your shop a few weeks ago. He went to see you, and you said you had no memory of it."

I paused to give him a chance to comment, but he offered none. His small tidy face displayed no reaction whatever.

I went on. "Of course I could raise my voice and get tough. I could say that it's unbelievable that you recently had an item as unusual as that in your shop but don't remember anything about it. You could say it may be unbelievable but it's true. Then I could say that your memory will have to be warmed up, and since I have no way of applying heat I'll have to turn it over to someone who has, Inspector Cramer of the Homicide Squad, though I would hate to do that."

I leaned back, at ease. "So I don't say it. I would rather put it to you on the merits. That boy was deliberately murdered by someone he had done no harm to. That was five days ago, and no trail has been found. Possibly one never will be found unless we can find the woman who was driving that car. She was wearing spider earrings, and apparently only one pair like that has ever been seen in New York, and it was seen in your window less than a month ago. I ask you, Mr. Gerster, does that have no effect on your memory?"

He passed the tip of his tongue over his lips. "You make it very difficult, Mr. Goodwin."

"Not me. The man who killed Pete made it difficult."

"Yes, of course. I knew nothing about that. I don't usually read about murders in newspapers. I did read a little about the death of Mrs. Fromm, including the detail that she was wearing spider earrings. You're quite right; they were unique. A man in Paris who picks up oddities for me included that one pair in a shipment which I received late in April. They were made by Lercari."

"You put them in your window?"

"That's right. This afternoon, when that man asked—what did you say his name is?

"Cather."

"Yes. When he asked about them I preferred not to remember. I suspected that he was a policeman engaged in the investigation of Mrs. Fromm's death, though I didn't know why the earrings were important, and I have a deep aversion to any kind of notoriety. It would be very unpleasant to see my name in a headline. I shall be most grateful if you can keep it from appearing, but I ask for no

promise. If any public testimony is required it will have to
be given. I sold the earrings in the afternoon of Monday,
May eleventh. A woman passing by saw them in the window and came in and bought them. She paid one hundred
and forty dollars, with a check. It was Mrs. Damon
Fromm."

It would have been an experience to play poker with that
bird. I asked, "No doubt about it?"

"None. The check was signed 'Laura Fromm,' and I
recognized her from pictures I had seen. I felt compelled to
tell you this, Mr. Goodwin, after what you told me about
the murder of that boy, though I realize that it won't help
any, since Mrs. Fromm was the woman in the car and she
is dead."

I could have told him that Mrs. Fromm was not the
woman in the car, but I had promised my grandmother that
I would never spout just to show people how much I knew,
so I skipped it. I thanked him and told him I didn't think
it would be necessary for his name to appear in headlines,
and got up to go. When, at the door, I extended a hand
and he took it courteously, his face had precisely the same
expression as when he had first confronted me.

Orrie rejoined me down in the lobby. He waited till we
were out on the sidewalk, in the drizzle again, to ask, "Did
you crack him?"

"Sure, nothing to it. He said he would have been glad to
tell you this afternoon but he caught you stashing a bracelet
in your pocket. Mrs. Fromm bought them May eleventh."

"I'll be damned. Where does that leave us?"

"Not my department. Wolfe does the thinking. I just
run errands that you have flubbed."

We flagged a taxi on Central Park West, and he went
downtown with me.

Wolfe was in the office looking at television, which gives
him a lot of pleasure. I have seen him turn it on as many as
eight times in one evening, glare at it from one to three
minutes, turn it off, and go back to his book. Once he made
me a long speech about it which I may record some day. As
Orrie and I entered he flipped the switch.

I told him. At the end I added, "I admit I took a risk. If
the boy had been not his son but a nephew he would like
to choke, I would have been sunk. I wish to recommend

that if we peddle this to the cops we leave his name out. And Orrie wants to know where this leaves us."

He grunted. "So do I. Saul phoned. He has started something, but he doesn't know what."

"I told you I saw him at the Assadip office."

"Yes. His name is Leopold Heim and he is living at a cheap hotel on First Avenue—it's here on my pad. He had a brief talk with Miss Wright, and one with her assistant, a Mr. Chaney. He appealed to them for help. He entered the country illegally and is in terror of being caught and deported. They told him that they cannot be accessory to a violation of law and advised him to consult a lawyer. When he said he knew no lawyer they gave him the name of Dennis Horan. That finnan haddie was too salty, and I'm thirsty. Will you have some beer, Orrie?"

"Yes, thanks, I will."

"Archie?"

"No, thank you. Beer likes me, but I don't like it."

He pressed a button on the rim of his desk and resumed. "Saul went to Mr. Horan's office and told him of his plight. Horan questioned him at length, taking many notes, and said that he would look into it as soon as possible and that Saul would hear from him. Saul went to his hotel room and stayed all afternoon. At six o'clock he went out for something to eat, and returned. Shortly before eight he had a caller, a man. The man gave no name. He said he had been aware for some time of Saul's predicament, and he sympathized with him and wanted to help. Since both the police and the FBI had to be dealt with, it would be costly. He estimated that the total amount required to prevent either exposure or harassment might go as high as ten thousand dollars."

He opened a drawer to get the gold opener, which bore an inscription from an ex-client, opened one of the bottles Fritz had brought, and poured.

When Fritz had opened Orrie's bottle, Wolfe continued, "Of course Saul protested in despair that it was impossible for him to procure such a sum. The man was prepared to make concessions. He said that it need not be paid in a lump; that weekly or monthly installments would be acceptable; that Saul could have twenty-four hours to explore expedients; and that an attempt to clear out would be disastrous. He said he would return at the same hour tomorrow, and left. Saul followed him. To attempt such a feat, following such a man in those circumstances, would of course be foolhardy for the most highly skilled operative, and even for Saul I would think it hazardous, but he managed it. He followed him to a restaurant on Third Avenue near Fourteenth Street. The man is now in the restaurant, eating. Saul phoned from across the street twenty minutes ago."

Wolfe drank beer. I had intended, when he was finished, to mix myself a healthy tall one to counteract the memory of the cold drizzle, but now I vetoed it. I could see Saul, and feel with him, in some little hole out of the drizzle, on Third Avenue, keeping his eyes peeled across the street past the El pillars, hoping to God his man wasn't phoning some pal to come for him in a car. Since it was Saul, the chances were that he already had a taxi parked down the block, but even so . . .

"I can take the sedan," I suggested, "and run Orrie over to Saul, and I'll lay back with the car. We three could hang onto Houdini."

Orrie gulped his beer down, stood up, and rumbled, "Let's go."

"I suppose so." Wolfe was frowning. Men willing, even eager, to go outdoors and brave the hubbub of the streets always discomposed him. At night, so much the worse; and at night in the rain it was outlandish. He sighed. "Go ahead."

The phone rang. He didn't reach for it, so I took it at my desk. "Nero Wolfe's residence, Archie Goodwin speak—"

"This is Fred, Archie. The boss ought to hear it too."

"Can you make it snappy?"

"No, it'll take a while, and I'm going to need you. I'm up—"

"Hold it a second." I turned. "It's Fred, and he sounds hot. You go on. The best bet on a taxi is Tenth Avenue. If Fred doesn't need me worse than Saul I'll join you soon. If he does I won't."

Wolfe gave Orrie the address, and he beat it, and Wolfe picked up his phone.

I told the receiver, "Okay, Fred, Mr. Wolfe is on."

Wolfe demanded, "Where are you?"

"In a booth in a drugstore on Ninth Avenue. Fifty-fifth Street. I think I'm onto something. This morning I saw that guy at the *Gazette* that Archie sent me to, and he gave me a lot of stuff on Matthew Birch. Birch had several personal habits to choose from, but his main hangout was a dump on Ninth Avenue, Danny's Bar and Grill, between Fifty-fourth and Fifty-fifth. Danny's name is Pincus, and he runs a book. The place didn't open until eleven, and it was dead the first hour, and Danny didn't show until after one. I didn't camp, but I was in and out, asking everybody I saw about Birch. Of course the cops have been there often the past few days, and they probably thought I was just one more, until finally I decided what the hell. I told a little group that my name was O'Connor, and what was eating me about Birch was that I had been told that my wife had been seen in a car with him last Tuesday afternoon, not many hours before he was killed. A dark gray Cadillac with a Connecticut plate. I said the car had been parked in front of Danny's Bar and Grill."

Wolfe grunted. "That was too specific."

"I guess it was, but I was playing for a rise, and you said I was to go on your assumption. And I got the rise. Most of them wasn't interested, except to tell me to forget it and get a new wife, but afterward one of them took me to a corner and wanted to know things. He was sharp, and I did the best I could. Finally he said it looked like I had a bum steer, but there was a guy that could give me the lowdown on Birch if anybody could, and if I wanted to see this guy a good time would be between nine-thirty and ten tonight, there at Danny's. A guy named Lips Egan."

"It is now nine-twenty-eight."

"I know it is. I was going to blow in right after nine-thirty, but I got to thinking. You ever hear of Lips Egan, Archie?"

"Not that I remember."

"I think I have. I think he used to beat carpets for Joe Slocum on the waterfront. If this is him maybe I showed too many cards and I'm going to be called, and I thought you might want to be around, but if you don't I can go ahead and play it."

"Go ahead and play it."

"Right." He didn't sound enthusiastic.

"But wait till I get there. Which side of the avenue is Danny's on?"

"West."

"Okay. I'm leaving now. I'll take the sedan. When you see me park across the street, go on into Danny's and keep your date. I'll stay in the car until I hear you scream or they roll your corpse out. If you leave with company I'll tail. If you leave alone head downtown and keep going, and as soon as I make sure you're loose I'll pick you up. Got it?"

"Yeah. How do I play him?"

"As Mr. Wolfe says, you got specific. You've bought it, Mr. O'Connor, so hang onto it. I'll find you a new wife."

"Any new instructions, Mr. Wolfe?"

"No. Proceed."

We hung up. From the drawer where I had put them on returning, I got a gun and holster and put them on. Wolfe sat scowling at me. Physical commotion and preparations for it irritate him, but as a practicing detective he defers to the necessity of putting people—me, for instance—in situations where they may get plugged or knifed or shoved off a cliff. In view of his distaste for such doings it's damn generous of him. I got an old hat and raincoat from the hall closet and left.

After getting the sedan from the garage around the corner, I crossed to Tenth Avenue and headed uptown. The drizzle was worse, if anything, and the mist thicker, but the staggered lights on Tenth Avenue keep you crawling anyhow. Turning right on Fifty-sixth, and again on Ninth Avenue, I made for the left side and slowed. There was a drugstore at the corner of Fifty-fifth. Ahead, across the street, a neon in a window said: DANNY'S BAR & GRILL. I rolled to the curb and stopped before I was even with Danny's, killed the engine, and cranked the right window down so I could see through the weather. In half a minute Fred appeared on the opposite side, proceeded to Danny's, and entered. It was 9:49.

Leaning back comfortably, through the open window I had a good view of Danny's except when passing cars intervened, and there weren't many. I decided to wait half an hour, until 10:19, before crossing the street and entering to see if Fred was still intact, but I didn't have to sweat it out that long. The dash clock said only two minutes past ten when Fred emerged with a man about half his size. The man had his right hand in his pocket and was at Fred's left elbow, so for a second I thought it was the old convoy game, but then Fred moseyed across the sidewalk, and the man headed uptown.

Fred stood at the curb, giving no sign, and I sat tight. The man turned left on Fifty-fifth. Three minutes passed, Fred standing and me sitting, and then a car came out of Fifty-fifth, turned into the avenue, and stopped where Fred was. The driver was Fred's companion, and he was alone. Fred got in beside him, and the car rolled.

With my engine still warm, there was nothing to it. I have good night eyes, and even in the drizzle I could give him a full block, and with Ninth Avenue wide and one-way I could keep over to my side, out of the range of his mirror. But I had barely catalogued those points in my favor when he left the avenue, swinging right into Forty-seventh Street. I made a diagonal across the bow of a thousand-ton truck, and the turn. He was on ahead. At Tenth Avenue a red light stopped him, and I braked to a crawl. When the light changed he turned uptown on Tenth, and I just did make the corner in time to see him swing, in the middle of the block, into the entrance of a garage. By the time I floated past he had disappeared inside. I went on by, turned into Forty-eighth, parked a foot beyond the building line, got out, and walked across the avenue to the west side.

The sign said NUNN'S GARAGE. It was an old brick building of three stories—nothing remarkable one way or another. I moved along to an entranceway across from it, stepped in out of the rain, and took a survey. The light inside was dim, and I couldn't see far into the entrance. On the two upper floors there was no light at all. The only adequate light was in a small room to the right of the entrance with two windows. In it were two desks and some chairs, but no people. When I had stood there ten minutes and still no sign of anyone, I decided that I didn't like it and it would be a good idea to try to find out why.

After going to the corner and crossing the avenue and coming back on the other side, I stopped smack in the middle of the entrance for a look. No one was in sight, but of course there could have been several platoons deployed among the congregation of cars and buses. I slipped in and to the left, behind a delivery truck, and stood and listened. There were faint sounds of movements, and then somewhere in the rear someone started to whistle "Oh, What a Beautiful Mornin'." As the whistler came nearer, off to the right, I edged around to the end of the truck. He finished his tune, but his footsteps were just as good on the concrete floor. He kept to the right—his left—almost to the entrance, and then a door opened and closed. He had gone into the office.

I moved fast but quietly, over nearly to the wall and then toward the rear through the maze of vehicles. When bumpers touched I detoured rather than risk a loose bolt under my weight. Halfway back I saw an objective, wooden stairs going up near the corner, and I made for it, but as I approached I became aware of a better objective. There were also steps going down, and up through the opening came the sound of voices. One of them was was Fred's. I went and stood at the top of the steps but couldn't catch any words.

There's only one way to reconnoiter in such a situation without exposing your feet and legs before your eyes have a chance. I lay down on my left side with my shoulder above the first step, gripped the upright with my right hand, and gently inched down until my eye was level with the basement ceiling. At first I saw nothing but another maze of cars and parts of cars, fading into darkness, but as I twisted my head around, nearly breaking my neck, I saw and heard that the voices were coming through a doorway in a partition that was apparently one wall of a built-in room. The door was open, but people in the room couldn't see the stairs unless they came to the door for a look.

I got to my feet and went downstairs, though not that fast. All you can do on a wooden stair is keep to the side, put your weight on each step a little at a time, and hope to God it was a good carpenter. I made it. The basement floor was concrete. I navigated it, now as silently as silence, across to the first car at the right, and behind it, and then slipped along to the next car, and the next. There, crouched in shadow, I could look straight into the room and hear their words. They were seated at a bare wooden table in the middle of the room, the little guy on the far side, facing me, and Fred at the left, in profile. Fred's hands were on the table. So were the little guy's, but he had a gun in one of his. I wondered how he got it staged that way, since Fred was not paralyzed, but that could wait. I got my gun from the holster, and it felt good in my hand. With the car to rest on, I could have picked any square inch on him.

He was talking. "Naw, I'm not like that. A guy that plugs a man just because he likes to feel the trigger work, he's goin' to get into trouble someday. Hell, I'd just as soon not shoot anybody. But, like I told you, Lips Egan don't like to talk to a man with a gun on him, and that's his privilege. He ought to be here any minute. Why I'm makin' all this speech—keep your hands still—I'm goin' to lift yours now, and you're big enough to break me up, so don't get any idea that I never would pull a trigger. Here in this basement we could have a shooting gallery. Maybe we will."

From the way he held the gun, firm and steady but not tight, he was a damn liar. He did like to feel the trigger work. He kept it firm and steady while he pushed his chair back, got erect, and stepped around back of Fred. From behind a man it's a little awkward to take a gun from under his left armpit with your left hand, but he did it very neatly and quickly. I saw Fred's jaw clamp, but except for that he took it like a gentleman. The man backed up a step, took a look at Fred's gun, nodded approvingly, dropped it into his side pocket, went back to his chair, and sat.

"Was you ever in Pittsburgh, Pennsylvania?" he asked.

"No," Fred said.

"I met a guy there once that made his own cattridges. I've never saw nothin' like it. He claimed his own powder mixture had more zip, but that was all hooey; he was a goddam maniac, that's all it was. If I ever found myself falling for a nutty idea like that I'd quit and hoe beans. Sure enough, a coupla years later I heard that this guy got it out in St. Louis, Missouri. I guess he musta forgot to put in the zip."

He laughed. Until then I had had no special personal feeling toward him, but that laugh was objectionable.

"Was you ever in St. Louis, Missouri?" he asked.

"No," Fred said.

"Neither was I. I understand it's on the Mississippi River. I'd like to see that goddam river. A guy told me once there's alligators in it, but I'd have to see 'em to believe 'em. About eight years ago I—"

A buzzer sounded—inside the room, I thought. A long buzz, then two short, close together, then another long. The man sidled to the wall, keeping his eyes and the gun on Fred, got his thumb on a button, and pressed it. It looked like one short, two long, and one short. Then he circled to the door and stood straddling the sill, facing the stairs, but with Fred well in range. In a moment there were footsteps overhead, and then the feet appeared on the stairs, descending. I ducked low, behind the car. It would be natural for a new arrival to glance around, and I wasn't ready to join the party.

"Hello, Mort."

"Hello, Lips. We been waiting."

"Is he clean?"

"Yeah, he had a S and W under his arm takin' his tempachure."

I stayed down until the newcomer's steps had crossed to the door and entered, then slowly came up until one eye reached the glass of the car's door. Mort had circled back to his former position and was standing beside the chair. Lips Egan stood across the table from Fred. He was fairly husky, with saggy shoulders, and was gray all over except for his blue shirt—gray suit, gray tie, gray face, and some gray in his dark hair. The tip of his nose tilted up a little.

"Your name's O'Connor?" he asked.

"Yes," Fred said.

"What's this about Matt Birch and your wife?"

"Someone told me they saw her in a car with him last Tuesday afternoon. I think maybe she was cheating on me. Then he got killed that night."

"Did you kill him?"

Fred shook his head. "I never heard about her being with him until yesterday?"

"Where were they seen?"

"The car was parked in front of Danny's. That's why I went there."

"What kind of a car?"

"Dark gray Caddy sedan, Connecticut plate. Look, all I want is about my wife. I just want to check her. This man,

Mort, whoever he is, he told me you might be able to help me."

"Yeah, I might be. Where's his stuff, Mort?"

"I didn't go through him, Lips. I was waitin' for you. I just took his gun."

"Let's see his stuff."

Mort told Fred, "Go hug the wall."

Fred sat. "First," he said, "about that name O'Connor. I told you that because I didn't want to use mine, my wife being in it. My name's Durkin, Fred Durkin."

"I said go hug the wall. There back of you."

Fred moved. After he had gone three paces I would have had to edge to the right to keep him in view, and look over the hood, and there was no point in risking it. Mort disappeared too. Faint sounds came, and after a little Mort's voice, "Stay where you are," and then he backed into view and took an assortment of objects from his pockets, putting them on the table. They were the usual items of a man's cargo, but among them I recognized the yellow envelope which held the photos I had delivered to Fred the day before.

Lips Egan, going through the pile, concentrated on that and the wallet and notebook. He took his time with the photos. When he spoke his voice was quite different. Not that it had been sociable, but now it was nasty. "His name's Fred Durkin, and he's a private dick."

"He is? The dirty bastard."

You might have thought Egan had said he was a dope peddler. He did say, "Get him back in the chair."

Mort issued a command, and Fred returned into view. He lowered himself into the chair and spoke. "Look, Egan, a private dick has his private life. I heard that my wife—"

"Can it. Who you working for?"

"I'm telling you. I wanted to check—"

"I said can it. Where did you get these pictures?"

"That's another matter. That's just business."

"There's one of Birch. Where'd you get 'em?"

"I thought I might get a line on the murder of that Mrs. Fromm and pull something."

"Who you working for?"

"No one. I'm telling you. For myself."

"Nuts. Give me the gun, Mort, and get some cord and the pliers."

Mort handed the gun over, went to a chest of drawers in the rear and opened one, and returned with a brown ball of heavy cord and a pair of pliers. The pliers were medium-sized and had something wrapped around the jaws, but I couldn't tell what. He came up behind Fred. "Put your hands back here."

Fred didn't move.

"Do you want to get slammed with your own gun? Put your paws back."

Fred obeyed. Mort unrolled a length of cord, cut it off with a knife, went down on his knees, did a thorough job of tying Fred's wrists, and wrapped the ends of the cord around the rung of the chair and tied them. Then he picked up the pliers. I couldn't see what he did with them, but I didn't need to.

"Does that hurt?" he asked.

"No," Fred said.

Mort laughed. "You be careful. You're goin' to answer some questions. If you get excited and start jerkin' you're apt to lose a finger, so watch it. All set, Lips."

Egan was seated across from Fred, with the hand that held the gun resting on the tabletop. "Who you working for, Durkin?"

"I told you, Egan, myself. If you'll just tell me if you saw my wife with Birch, yes or no, that's all there is to it."

Fred finished his sentence, but he gave a little gasp and went stiff in the middle of it. I suppose I could have stood it a little while, maybe up to two minutes, and it would have been educational to see how much Fred could take; but if he got a finger broken, Wolfe would have to pay the doctor bill, and I like to protect the interests of my employer. So I slipped to the right, rested the gun on the hood, drew a bead on Egan's hand holding the gun, and fired. Then I was around the front of the car on the jump, with all the muscle I had, and springing for the door.

I had seen Mort drop Fred's gun into his left pocket, and unless he was a switch-hitter I figured that should give me about three seconds, especially since he was down on his knees. But he didn't wait to get up. By the time I made the door he had flung himself around behind Fred. I dropped flat and from there, looking underneath the seat of Fred's chair I saw his left hand leaving his pocket with the gun in it. I had dropped with my gun hand extended in front of me along the floor, and I pulled the trigger. Then I was on my feet again, or rather in the air, coming down behind Fred's chair. Mort, still on his knees, was reaching for the gun on the floor two feet away, with his right hand. I kicked him in the belly, saw him start to crumple, and jerked around for Egan. He was ten feet toward the rear, stooping over to pick up his gun. If I had known what his condition was I would have stood and watched. As I learned later, the bullet hadn't touched him. It had hit the cylinder of the gun, tearing it from his grip, and he had been holding it so tight that his hand had been numbed, and now he was trying to pick up the gun and couldn't. Not knowing that, I went for him, slammed him against the wall, picked up the gun, heard commotion behind me, and wheeled.

Fred had somehow got himself, chair and all, across to where his gun was, and was sitting there with both his feet on it. Mort was on the floor, writhing.

I stood and panted, shaking all over.

"Jesus H. Moses," Fred said.

I couldn't speak. Egan was standing against the wall, rubbing his right hand with his left one. Mort's left hand was bleeding. I stood and panted some more. When the shaking had about stopped I put Mort's gun in my pocket, got out my knife, and went to Fred and cut the cord.

He took his feet off of his gun, picked it up, stood, and tried to grin at me. "You go lie down and take a nap."

"Yeah." I had about caught up on breathing. "That bird upstairs must be curious, and I'll go up and see. Keep these two quiet."

"Let me go. You've done your share."

"No, I'll take a look. Watch these babies."

"Don't worry."

I left the room, went to the foot of the stairs, and stood and listened. Nothing. With the gun in my hand and my head tilted back, I started up, slow and easy. I doubted if the garage man was much a menace, but he could have phoned for help, and also Lips Egan might not have come alone. Having just proved I was a double-breasted hero before a witness, I intended to stay alive to enjoy the acclaim. So when my eyes were up to the level of the floor above I stopped again to look and listen. Still nothing. I went on up and was on the concrete. The route I had come by was as good as any, and I moved into the throng of cars and trucks. Halting every few feet to cock my ears, I was about halfway to the entrance where I became aware that someone was there, not far off to the right. That often happens. It's barely possible it comes by smell sometimes, but I think you get it either through your ears or your eyes, keyed up as they are, so faint you only feel it. Anyhow someone was there. I stopped and crouched.

I stuck there, huddled against a truck, straining my eyes and ears, for ten hours. Okay, make it ten minutes. It was enough. I began moving, one foot per minute, toward the rear of the truck. I wanted to see around the back end. It took forever, but I finally made it. I stood and listened and then stretched my neck and got my eye just beyond the edge of the truck's corner. A man was standing there an arm's length away, looking straight at me. Before he could move I stuck my head clear out.

"Hello, Saul," I whispered.

"Hello, Archie," he whispered back.

12 I moved around the corner of the truck. "Where's the floor man?" I whispered.

"Orrie's got him over back of the office, tied up. Orrie's sticking near the entrance."

I quit whispering. "Hooray. I'll recommend you for a raise. You tailed Lips Egan here?"

"I don't know his name, but we tailed him here. Then we thought we'd come in out of the rain, and the floor man spotted us, and we had to wrap him up. Then we heard two shots, and I started back to inquire, and I smelled you and stopped to think. You certainly are a noisy walker."

"So are you. I never heard such a din. Talk as loud as you

want to. Egan is down in the basement with a friend, and Fred's there keeping them out of mischief."

Saul is hard to surprise, but that did it. "You mean it?"

"Come and see."

"How did you do it? Radar?"

"Oh, you'll usually find me where I'm needed. Guts Goodwin. I'll tell you later; we've got some work to do. Let's have a word with Orrie."

I led the way, and he followed. Orrie was standing not far in from the entrance. At sight of me his eyes popped. "What the hell! How come?"

"Later. Fred's downstairs holding two guys. Saul and I are going down for a game of pinochle. Any kind of specimens are apt to turn up here, so watch it. Is the floor man okay?"

"Saul and I okayed him."

"Right. Our lives are in your hands, so go to sleep. Come on, Saul."

In the room in the basement Fred had the situation in hand. He was on the chair formerly occupied by Mort, facing the door. Mort was stretched out on his back over by the left wall, with his ankles tied, and Egan was nearby, sitting on the floor, propped against the wall, with his ankles likewise. Saul's appearance with me caused a little stir.

"So that's what kept you so long," Fred commented, not pleased. "Do we need an army?"

Lips Egan muttered something.

"No," I told Fred, "I didn't send for him. He was upstairs, came on Egan's tail. Orrie's up there too, and we own the place."

"I'll be damned. Let me see Mort's gun."

I took it from my pocket and handed it to him, and he inspected it. "Yeah, I thought so, here on the cylinder. You didn't touch Egan. Mort's hand is a little messy, but I put a handkerchief around it, and it'll keep a while. You kicked his stomach up to his throat, and I tell him he ought to sit up so it can slide down again, but he wants to rest."

I crossed to Mort, squatted, and took a look. His color wasn't very good, but his eyes were open and not glassy. I gave his abdomen a few gentle pokes and asked if it hurt. Without wincing, he told me to go do something vulgar, so I got erect, moved on to Egan, and stood looking down at him. Saul joined me.

"My name's Archie Goodwin," I told him. "I work for Nero Wolfe. So do my friends here. That's what you wanted Fred Durkin to spill, so now that's out of the way and it's our turn. Who are you working for?"

He didn't reply. He didn't even have the courtesy to look at me, but stared at his ankles. I said to Saul, "I'll empty him, and you do the other one," and we proceeded. I took my collection to the table, and Saul brought his. There was nothing worth framing in Mort's contribution except a driver's license in the name of Mortimer Ervin, but in Egan's pile was an item that showed real promise—a thick looseleaf notebook about four by seven, with a hundred pages, and each page had a dozen or so names and addresses. I flipped through it. The names seemed to be all flavors, and the addresses all in the metropolitan area. I handed it to Saul, and while he was taking a look I crossed to the chest of drawers, the only piece of furniture in the room that could have held anything, and went through it. I found nothing of any interest.

Saul called to me, "The last entry here is Leopold Heim and the address."

I went and glanced at it. "That's interesting. I didn't notice it." I slipped the book in my side pocket, the one that didn't have Mort's gun in it, and walked over to Egan. He glanced up at me, a really mean glance, and then returned to his ankles.

I addressed him. "If there's a thousand names in that book, and if each one donated ten grand, that would be ten million bucks. I suppose that's exaggerated, but discount it ninety per cent and you've still got a nice little sum. Do you care to comment?"

No reply.

"We haven't got all night," I said, "but I ought to explain that while we disapprove of blackmail rackets, especially this kind, that's not what we're working on. We're on a murder, or maybe I should say three murders. If I ask about your racket it's only to get at a murder. For instance, was Matthew Birch in with you?"

His chin jerked up, and he blurted at Saul, "You dirty little squirt!"

I nodded. "Now that's out, and you'll feel better. Was Birch in with you?"

"No."

"Who gave you the tip on Leopold Heim?"

"Nobody."

"How much is your cut of the dough, and who gets the rest?"

"What dough?"

I shrugged. "So you ask for it, huh? Take his arms, Saul."

I got his ankles, and we lugged him across to the opposite wall and put him down alongside a little stand that held a telephone. He started to wriggle around to prop himself against the wall, but I told Saul, "Keep him flat while I see if this phone's connected," and lifted the receiver and dialed a number. After only two whirrs a voice said, "Nero Wolfe speaking."

"Archie. I'm just testing a phone."

"It's midnight. Where the devil are you?"

"We're here together, all four of us, operating a garage on Tenth Avenue. We have customers waiting, and I'm too busy to talk. You'll hear from us later."

"I'm going to bed."

"Sure. Sleep tight."

I cradled the receiver, lifted the instrument, slid the stand along the wall out of the way, put the instrument on the floor a foot from Egan's shoulder as he lay, and called to Fred, "Bring that ball of cord."

He came with it, asking, "The crisscross?"

"Right. A piece about eight feet long."

While he was cutting it off I explained to Egan. "I don't know whether you've been introduced to this or not. It's a scientific method of stimulating the vocal cords. If and when you find you don't like it, the phone's right there by you. You can dial either police headquarters, Canal six-two-thousand, or the Sixteenth Precinct, Circle six-oh-four-one-six, which is right near here, but don't try dialing any other number. If you ring the cops we'll turn off the science and you can tell them anything you want to without interference. That's guaranteed. All right, Saul, pin his shoulders. Here, Fred."

We squatted by Egan's ankles, one on each side. It isn't complicated, but it's a little delicate if the patient has brittle bones. First you double the cord and noose it around the left ankle. Then you cross the legs, the right one over the left one, and work the toe of the right shoe under the left heel and around to the right side of it. For that the knees have to be bent. Pull the right ankle down as nearly even with the left ankle as possible, wind the doubled cord around them both, three tight turns, take a half-hitch and you've got it. If you grab the free ends of the cord and give a healthy yank straight down, away from the feet, the patient will probably pass out, so you don't do that. Even a gentle yank is not good technique. You merely hold the cord taut to maintain the tension. Meanwhile your colleague keeps the patient's shoulders in place, though even without him you have complete control. If you doubt it, try it.

With Saul at the shoulders and Fred at the end of the cord, I brought a chair over, sat, and watched Egan's face. He was trying to keep it from registering. "This hurts you more than it does me," I told him, "so any time you want to call the cops say so. If your legs are too uncomfortable to turn over to dial I'll cut the cord. A little tighter, Fred, just a little. Was Birch in on your racket?"

I waited ten seconds. His face was twisting, and he was breathing fast. "Did you see Birch in that car Tuesday afternoon?"

His eyes were shut, and he was trying to move his shoulders. Another ten seconds. "Who gave you the tip on Leopold Heim?"

"I want the cops," he said hoarsely.

"Right. Cut it, Fred."

Instead of cutting it, he undid the half-hitch, unwrapped the wind, and eased the left toe back under the heel. Egan started to pump his knees, slowly and carefully.

"No calisthenics," I told him. "Dial."

He turned on his side, lifted the receiver, and started to dial. Saul and I both watched. He hit the right holes, CA 6-2000. I heard him get an answer, and he said, "Police headquarters?" Then he dropped the receiver back in place and said to me, "You sonofabitch, you would?"

"Certainly," I told him, "I guaranteed it. Before we stimulate you again, a couple of points. You get one more chance to call the cops, that all. You could keep this up all night. Second, it might be slick to come across now. If you're taking it for granted that your address book will get to the cops anyway, you're wrong. I'll give it to Mr. Wolfe, and he's working on a murder, and I don't think he'll feel like turning all those people over to the law. That's not his lookout. I make no promise, but I'm telling you. All right, Fred. Pin him, Saul."

That time we reserved it, crossing his left leg over his right, and we made the turns slightly tighter. Fred took the cord ends, and I returned to the chair. The reaction came quicker and stronger. In ten seconds his face began to twist. In ten more his forehead and neck went wet with sweat. His gray face got grayer, and his eyes opened and started to bulge. I was about to tell Fred to ease it a little when he gasped, "Let up!"

"Off a little, Fred. Just hold it. Was Birch in on the racket?"

"Yes!"

"Who's the boss?"

"Birch was. Take that cord off!"

"In a minute. It's better than pliers. Who's the boss now?"

"I don't know."

"Nuts. The cord had better stay a while. Did you see Birch in a car with a woman last Tuesday afternoon?"

"Yes, but it wasn't parked in front of Danny's."

"Slightly tighter, Fred. Where was it?"

"Going down Eleventh Avenue in the Fifties."

"A dark gray Caddy sedan with a Connecticut plate?"

"Yes."

"Was it Birch's car?"

"I never saw it before. But Birch worked with a hot-car gang too, and of course that Caddy was hot. Everything Birch had a hand in was hot."

"Yeah, he's dead now, so why not? Who was the woman with him?"

"I don't know. I was across the street and didn't see. Take the cord off! No more until it's off!"

He was breathting fast again, and his face was grayer, so I told Fred to give him a recess. When his legs had been unwound Egan thought he would bend them, then

thought he would straighten them, then decided to post-
pone trying to move them.

I continued. "Didn't you recognize the woman?"

"No."

"Could you identify her?"

"I don't think so. They just went by."

"What time Tuesday afternoon?"

"Around half-past six, maybe a little later."

I would take that, anyhow on consignment. Pete Drossos
had said it was a quarter to seven when the woman in the
car had told him to get a cop. I almost hated to ask the
next question for fear of Egan disqualifying himself by
answering it wrong.

"Who was driving, Birch?"

"No, the woman. That surprised me. Birch wasn't a guy
to have a woman driving him."

I could have kissed the louse. He had made it twenty to
one on Wolfe's hit-or-miss assumption. I had a notion to
get the photos of Jean Estey, Angela Wright, and Claire
Horan from Fred's envelope and ask Egan if the woman
in the car had resembled one of them, but skipped it. He
had said he couldn't identify her, and he certainly wasn't
going to take on more load than he already had.

I asked him, "Who do you deliver the dough to?"

"Birch."

"He's dead. Who to now?"

"I don't know."

"I guess we took the cord off too soon. If Leopold Heim
had paid you the ten grand or any part of it, what would
you have done with it?"

"Held onto it until I got word."

"Word from whom?"

"I don't know."

I got up. "The cord, Fred."

"Wait a minute," Egan pleaded. "You asked me where I
got the tip on Leopold Heim. I got leads two ways, straight
from Birch, and on the phone. A woman would call and
give it to me."

"What woman?"

"I don't know. I've never seen her."

"How would you know it wasn't a trap? Just by her
voice?"

"I knew her voice, but there's a password."

"What is it?"

Egan tightened his lips.

"You won't be using it any more," I assured him, "so let's have it."

" 'Said a spider to a fly.' "

"What?"

"That's the password. That's how I got the lead on Leopold Heim. You asked who I would deliver dough to with Birch dead. I thought she would phone and tell me."

"Why didn't she tell you when she phoned you the lead on Heim?"

"I asked her, and she said she'd tell me later."

"What's her name?"

"I don't know."

"What number do you call her at?"

"I never call her. Birch was my contact. Now I wouldn't know how to get her."

"Phooey. We'll come back to that if we have to stimulate you. Why did you kill Birch?"

"I didn't kill him. I'm not a killer."

"Who did?"

"I don't know."

I sat down. "As I told you, what I'm interested in is murder. With that cord we could squeeze your guts out, but that wouldn't help us any; we just want facts, and facts we can check. If you didn't kill Birch and don't know who did, now tell me exactly how you've got it doped, and don't—"

A buzzer sounded. I left the chair. It went two short, one long, and one short. I said sharply, "Muzzle 'em." Saul pressed a palm over Egan's mouth, and Fred went to Mort. I stepped to the wall, to the button I had seen Mort use, and pushed it. Probably the one short, two long, and one short, wasn't the right answer this time, but it was as good as any ad lib. Then I left the room and, with my gun ready, stood three paces off from the foot of the stairs. I heard a voice up above, faintly, then silence, then footsteps, at first barely audible but getting louder. Then Orrie's voice came down. "Archie?"

"Yeah. Present."

"I'm bringing company."

"Fine. The more the merrier."

The steps reached the head of the stairs and started down. I saw well-shined black shoes, then well-pressed dark blue trouser legs, then a jacket to match, and to top it all the face of Dennis Horan. The face was very expensive. Behind him was Orrie with his gun visible.

"Hello there," I said.

He wasn't speaking, so I switched to Orrie. "How did he come?"

"In a car alone. He drove in, and I took it easy, not interested. He glanced at me but didn't say anything and went to a button on a pillar and pushed it. When a buzzer sounded I thought it was time to take a hand, so I showed my gun and told him to walk. Whoever pushed that buzzer may be—"

"That's all right, I did. Have you felt him?"

"No."

I went to Horan and patted him in the likely spots and some unlikely ones. "Okay. Go back up and tend to customers." Orrie went, and I sang out, "Saul! Take the muzzle off and tie his ankles and come here."

Horan started for the door of the room. I grabbed his arm and whirled him. He tried to pull away, and I gave him a good twist. "Don't think I'm not serious," I told him. "I know what number to call for an ambulance."

"Yes, it is serious," he agreed. His thin tenor needed oil. "Serious enough to finish you, Goodwin."

"Maybe, but right now I'm it, and it has gone to my head, so watch out." Saul came out. "This is Mr. Saul Panzer. Saul, this is Dennis Horan. We'll invite him to the conference later, but first I want to make a phone call. Take him over by the far wall. Don't disfigure him unless he insists on it. He's not armed."

I crossed to the room, entered, and shut the door. Fred was seated at the table massaging a finger, and the other two were as before. I pulled the little stand back to its place, picked up the phone and put it on the stand, seated myself, and dialed. This time it took more whirrs to get results, and then only a peevish mutter.

"Archie. I need advice."

"I'm asleep."

"Go splash your face with cold water."

"Good heavens. What is it?"

"As I told you, all four of us are here in a garage. We have two subjects in a room in the basement. One of them is a biped named Mortimer Ervin, who has probably got nothing for us. The other one is called Lips Egan. On his driver's license his first name is Lawrence. He's the article that called on Saul at his hotel, and Saul and Orrie tailed him here. He's a jewel. He had on him a notebook, now in my pocket, with about a thousand names and addresses of customers, and the last entry in it is Leopold Heim, so draw your own conclusions. We stimulated him some, and he claims that Matthew Birch was bossing the racket, but I haven't bought that. I have bought that he saw Birch in that Cadillac, Tuesday afternoon, with a woman driving. I have not bought that he didn't recognize her and couldn't identify her. Nor that—"

"Proceed with him. Why disturb me in the middle of it?"

"Because we've been disturbed. Dennis Horan drove in upstairs and gave a code signal to the basement on a buzzer, and Orrie took him and brought him down. He's out of earshot, but the other two are right here. I want your opinion on the kind and amount of stimulation to apply to a member of the bar. Of course he came to see Egan and he's in on the racket, but I haven't got it in writing."

"Is Mr. Horan bruised?"

"We've hardly touched him."

"Have you questioned him any?"

"No, I thought I'd call you."

"This is very satisfactory. Hold the wire while I wake up."

I did so. It was a full minute, maybe more, before his voice came again. "How are you arranged?"

"Fred and I are in the room in the basement with Ervin and Egan. Saul has Horan outside. Orrie's upstairs to receive visitors."

"Get Mr. Horan in and apologize to him."

"Oh, have a heart."

"I know, but he's a lawyer, and we won't give him cards to play. Has either Ervin or Egan shown a weapon?"

"Both. To Fred. They took his gun away, tied him in a chair, and were twisting his fingers around with pliers when I interrupted them."

"Good. Then you have them on two counts, attempted extortion from Saul and assault with a firearm on Fred. Here are your instructions."

He gave them to me. Some of it was too sketchy, and I asked him to elaborate. Finally I said I thought I had it. At the end he told me to hang on to Egan's notebook, mention it to no one, and put it in the safe as soon as I got home. I hung up, went and opened the door, and called to Saul to bring Horan in.

Horan's face was not so expressive. Apparently he had decided on a line, and it called for a deadpan. He took a chair like a lamb, showing no interest whatever in either Ervin or Egan beyond glances at the prostrate figures as he entered.

I addressed him. "If you'll excuse me, Mr. Horan, I have to say something to these two men. You listening, Ervin?"

"No."

"Suit yourself. You committed felonious assault on Fred Durkin with a loaded gun, and you committed battery on him with a pair of pliers. Are you listening, Egan?"

"I hear you."

"You also committed assault—with the gun I shot out of your hand. In addition, you attempted extortion from Saul Panzer, another felony. My own inclination would be to phone the cops to come and get you two birds, but I work for Nero Wolfe, and it's just possible he'll feel differently about it. He wants to ask you some questions, and I'm taking you both down to his place. If you prefer going to the station, say so, but that's your only alternative. If you try making a break you'll be surprised, or maybe you won't."

I turned to the lawyer. "As for you, Mr. Horan, I tender our sincere apologies. We were under quite a strain, having this run-in with these two characters, and Orrie Cather was a little too eager, and so was I. I just talked to Mr. Wolfe on the phone, and he said to give you his regrets for the way his employees treated you. I guess I should apologize for another little thing too—when I introduced Saul Panzer to you out there I forgot he had called at your office today under the name of Leopold Heim. That must have been confusing. That's all, unless you want to say something. Go on about your business, and I hope you won't hold this against us—no, wait a minute, I just got an idea."

I turned to Egan. "We want to be absolutely fair, Egan, and it just occurred to me that you might want a lawyer around while you're down at Mr. Wolfe's, and by coincidence this man is a lawyer. His name's Dennis Horan. I don't know whether he'd care to represent you, but you can ask him if you want to."

I thought, and still think, that that was one of Wolfe's neatest little notions, and I wouldn't have missed the look on their faces for a week's pay. Egan twisted his head around to see Horan, obviously to get a steer. But Horan himself needed a steer. The suggestion had caught him by surprise, and it had too many aspects. To say yes would be risky, since it would tie him to Egan, and he didn't know how much Egan had spilled. To say no would be just as risky, doubly risky, because Egan might think he was being ditched, and also because Egan was being taken for a session with Nero Wolfe and there was no telling how he would stand up. It was too damned complicated and important to answer right off the bat, and it was a treat to watch Horan blinking his long eyelashes and trying to preserve his deadpan while he worked on it.

Egan broke the silence. "I've got some cash on me for a retainer, Mr. Horan. I understand it's kind of a lawyer's duty to defend people in trouble."

"So it is, Mr. Egan." The tenor was squeezing through. "I'm very busy right now."

"Yeah, I'm pretty busy too."

"No doubt. Yes. Of course." Horan straightened his shoulders. "Very well. I'll see what I can do for you. We'll have to have a talk."

I grinned at him. "Any talking you do," I stated, "will have listeners. Let's go, boys. Untie 'em. Fred, bring the pliers along for a souvenir."

13 I need eight and a half hours' sleep and I prefer nine. Every morning when my bedside clock turns on the radio at seven-thirty I roll over to have it at the back of my ears. In a minute I roll over again, reach to turn it off, get comfortable, and try to figure that it's Sunday. But I know damn well Fritz will have my breakfast ready at 8:10. For two or three minutes I wrestle with the idea of getting him on the house phone to say I'll be a little late, then give up, kick the cover back, swing my legs around, get upright, and start to face realities.

That Tuesday morning was different. I had set the clock an hour earlier, for six-thirty, and when it clicked and the radio started one of those goddam cheerful morning jamborees I flipped the switch and got my feet to the floor in one desperate convulsion. I had been horizontal just two hours. I showered, shaved, combed and brushed, dressed, went downstairs, and entered the front room.

It was not a gay scene. Mortimer Ervin was stretched out on the carpet with his head resting on one of the cushions from the couch. Lips Egan was lying on the couch. Dennis Horan was in the upholstered armchair, rumpled but not relaxed. Saul Panzer was on a chair with its back to the window, his wards all in range without his having to overwork his eyes,

"Good morning," I said gloomily. "Breakfast will soon be served."

"This is insufferable," Horan squeaked.

"Then don't suffer it. I've told you at least five times you're free to go. As for them, it's de luxe. A couch and a soft carpet to rest on. Doc Vollmer, who left his bed at two in the morning to dress Mort's hand, is as good as they come. We're leaning over backwards. Mr. Wolfe thought you might feel he was taking an unfair advantage if he worked on them privately before notifying the law, so he didn't even get up to have a look at them. He stayed

117

isolated in his room, either in bed or pacing the floor, I can't say which. In your presence and hearing I phoned Manhattan Homicide at one-forty-seven a.m. and said that Mr. Wolfe had something important to tell Inspector Cramer personally and would appreciate a call from Cramer at his earliest convenience. As for your desire to be alone with your client, we couldn't possibly let a ruffian like Egan out of our sight. Cramer would give us hell. How are you, Saul?"

"Fine. I had three hours' sleep before I relieved Fred at five-thirty."

"You don't look it. I'll go see about breakfast."

While I was in the kitchen with Fritz, Fred came in, fully dressed, with a staggering piece of news. He and Orrie had been pounding their ears in the twins beds in the south room, which is on the same floor as mine, and had been aroused by the sound of tapping on the ceiling of the room below, which was Wolfe's. Fred had gone down to see, and had been told by Wolfe to send Orrie to him at once. I would have had to dig deep in my memory for a precedent of Wolfe doing any business whatever before he had his breakfast.

Fritz had his hands full with eight breakfasts to prepare and serve, not counting his own, but Fred and I cooperated by putting a table in the front room and conveying food and equipment. We ate in the kitchen, and were disposing of our share of corn muffins and broiled ham and honey when Orrie marched in and commanded Fritz, "Forget these bums and attend to me. I have to go on a mission, and I'm hungry. Archie, go get me five hundred bucks. While you're gone I'll swipe your chair. Also give me the name of that outfit with a bunch of guys that make phone calls for so much per thousand."

I kept my chair until my breakfast was down, including a second cup of coffee, so he had to perch on the stool. Then I filled his orders. It was useless to try to guess what he was going to do with the five hundred, but if any substantial part of it was for buying phone calls wholesale I might try doping that for practice. Since I had reported to Wolfe in full up in his room after depositing our guests downstairs, he knew everything I did, but no more. Who could be the likely candidates for a thousand phone calls? It couldn't be the people listed in Egan's customer book, for it was locked in the safe—I saw it there when I got the currency from the expense drawer—and Orrie hadn't asked for it. I filed the question in my mind for further consideration during spare moments, if I had any. It wasn't the first time Wolfe had sent one of the help on an errand without consulting me.

By eight o'clock Fritz had brought Wolfe's tray back down, and Orrie had left, and Fred and I had brought the breakfast things from the front room and were in the kitchen helping with the dishes, when the doorbell rang. I tossed the dishtowel to a table and went to the hall, and when I saw Inspector Cramer and Sergeant Purley Stebbins on the stoop I didn't have to keep them waiting while I sought instructions. I already had instructions, so, with a glance en route to make sure the door to the front room was closed, I went and opened up and welcomed them.

They stayed put. "We're on our way somewhere," Cramer rasped. "What do you want to tell me?"

"Nothing. Mr. Wolfe is the teller. Step in."

"I can't wait around for him."

"You won't have to. He's been anxiously expecting you for six hours."

They entered and headed for the office. As I entered behind them Cramer growled, "He's not here."

I ignored it, told them to be seated, went to my desk and buzzed Wolfe's room on the house phone, and told him who had arrived. Cramer got a cigar from a pocket, rolled it between his palms, inspected the end of it as if to see whether someone had dosed it with some rare and obscure poison, stuck it between his lips, and clamped his teeth on it. I had never seen him light one. Stebbins sat taking me in at a slant. He hated having his commanding officer coming there when a big murder case was sizzling, and I wouldn't bet that he wouldn't still have hated it even if he knew that we had the murderer, with ample evidence, wrapped up and waiting.

The sound of the descending elevator came, and in a moment Wolfe entered. He greeted the company with no enthusiasm, crossed to his desk, and before sitting down demanded, "What kept you so long? Mr. Goodwin phoned more than six hours ago. My house is full of questionable characters, and I want to get rid of them."

"Skip it," Cramer snapped. "We're in a hurry. What characters?"

Wolfe sat, taking his time to get arranged. "First," he said, "have you any comment about Miss Estey's charge that Mr. Goodwin offered to sell her a report of the conversation I had with Mrs. Fromm?"

"No. That's up to the District Attorney. You're stalling."

Wolfe shrugged. "Second, about the spider earrings. Mrs. Fromm bought them at a midtown shop on Monday afternoon, May eleventh. As you have doubtless discovered, there is probably no other pair like them in New York and never has been."

Stebbins got out his notebook. Cramer demanded, "Where did you get that?"

"By inquiry. I give you the fact; the way I got it is my affair. She saw them in a window, bought them, paid by check, and took them with her. Since you have access to her check stubs you can probably find the shop and verify this, but I can't imagine a sillier waste of time. I vouch for the fact, and reflection will show you that it is extremely significant."

"In what way?"

"No. Do your own interpreting. I supply only facts. Here's another. You know Saul Panzer."

"Yes."

"Yesterday he went to the office of the Association for the Aid of Displaced Persons, gave the name of Leopold Heim and as his address a cheap hotel on First Avenue, and talked both with Miss Angela Wright and a man named Chaney. He told them that he was in this country illegally and in fear of being exposed and deported, and asked for help. They said his plight was outside their field of activity, advised him to go to a lawyer, and gave him the name of Dennis Horan. He went and talked with Mr. Horan, and then went to his hotel. Shortly before eight o'clock in the evening a man arrived at his room and offered to protect him against exposure or harassment upon payment of ten thousand dollars. Mr. Panzer will give you all details. He was given twenty-four hours to scrape up all the money he could, and when the man left, Mr. Panzer followed him. He is pre-eminent at that."

"I know he is. Then what?"

"We'll shift to Mr. Goodwin. Before he proceeds I should explain that I had made an assumption about the man in the car with the woman last Tuesday when the woman told the boy to get a cop. I had assumed that the man was Matthew Birch."

Cramer's eyes widened. "Why Birch?"

"I don't have to expound it because it has been validated. It was Birch. Another fact."

"Show me. This one will have to be filled in good."

"By Mr. Goodwin. He'll get to it. Archie, start with Fred's phone call last evening and go on through."

I complied. Having known that this would be somewhere on the program, I had spent most of an hour carefully going over it, while I had been on guard duty in the front room from three-thirty to four-thirty, and had decided that only two major items should be omitted: the kind of stimulation used on Lips Egan, and Egan's notebook. The latter wouldn't be mentioned, and wasn't. Wolfe had said, during our session up in his room, that if it proved later to be essential evidence we would have to produce it, but not otherwise.

Except for those two items I delivered the crop. Stebbins started taking notes but quit halfway through. It was too much for him. I handed him Mort's gun and exhibited the pliers, which had black tape wrapped thick around the jaws to keep them from breaking skin and bruising flesh. When I finished, Cramer and Stebbins sat looking at each other.

Cramer turned to Wolfe. "This needs some sorting out."

"Yes," Wolfe agreed. "It does indeed."

Cramer turned to Stebbins. "Do we know this Egan?"

"I don't, but I've been on Homicide all my life."

"Get Rowcliff and tell him to get on him fast."

I left my chair, and Purley got in it and dialed. While he was phoning, Cramer sat holding his cigar in his fingers, frowning at it, and rubbing his lips with a knuckle of his other hand. It looked exactly as if he were trying to make up his mind whether to quit cigar-chewing. When Purley was through and back in his chair, Cramer looked at

Wolfe. "Horan's in it up to his neck, but we can't hold him now."

"I'm not holding him. He is voluntarily cleaving to his client."

"Yeah, I know. I hand you that one. It tagged Horan all right. If we can make Egan sing we've got it."

Wolfe shook his head. "Not necessarily the murderer. Possibly Egan knows as little about the murders as you do."

It was a dirty crack, but Cramer ignored it. "We'll give him a chance," he declared. "Plenty. I've got to sort this out. It's not absolutely tight that it was Birch in the car with the woman. Suppose it wasn't? Suppose the man in the car was one of the poor devils they had their hooks into. The woman was the one in the racket, the one that phones Egan the leads. She thought the man was going to kill her, so she told the boy to get a cop. Somehow she got out of it, but that night she got hold of Birch, who was running the racket, and killed him. Then he knew the boy could identify him—he might even have killed the woman, and her body hasn't been found—so the next day he killed the boy. Then he knew Mrs. Fromm was the head of that Association, so he killed her. My God, this makes it wide open, this racket and Horan in it. People like that are desperate, and there are thousands of them in New York —people here illegally and afraid of getting kicked out. They're soup for blackmailers. There must be a list somewhere of the ones these bastards were nicking, and I wish I had it. I would make it even money that the name of the murderer is on it. Would you?"

"No."

"Anything to be contrary. Why not?"

"You haven't done enough sorting, Mr. Cramer. But your snatching at a blackmail victim as the culprit shows that you're hard up. There have been three murders. Assuming, to keep it tidy, that there is only one murderer, have all the handy ones been eliminated?"

"No."

"Who has been?"

"Crossed off, nobody. Of course there are complications. For instance, Mrs. Horan says that Friday night her husband returned to the apartment ten minutes after he left with Mrs. Fromm to take her down to her car, and he went to bed and stayed there, but that's a wife corroborating a husband. If you're ready to nominate a candidate don't let me stop you. Have you got one?"

"Yes."

"The hell you have. Name him."

"The question was, have I a candidate, not am I ready to nominate. I may be ready in an hour, or in a week, but not now."

Cramer grunted. "Either you're grandstanding, which would be nothing new, or you're holding out. I admit you've made a haul—this racket, and Egan, and, by luck, Horan too—and much obliged. Okay. None of that names the murderer. What else? If you're after a deal, here I am. I'll give you anything and everything we've got, ask me anything you want to—of course that's what you're after—if you'll reciprocate and give me all you've got."

Stebbins made a noise and then tried to look as if he hadn't.

"That," Wolfe said, "is theoretically a fair and forthright proposal, but practically it's pointless. Because first, I've given you all I've got; and second, you have nothing I want or need."

Cramer and Stebbins gawked at him, both surprised and suspicious.

"You've already told me," Wolfe went on, "that no one has been eliminated, more than three days since Mrs. Fromm was killed. That will do for me. By now you have tens of thousands of words of reports and statements, and I admit it's possible that buried somewhere in them is a fact or a phrase I might think cogent, but even if you cart it all up here I don't intend to wade through it. For example, how many pages have you on the background and associates and recent comings and goings of Miss Angela Wright?"

"Enough," Cramer growled.

"Of course. I don't decry it. Such lines of inquiry often get you an answer, but manifestly in this case they haven't even hinted at one or you wouldn't be here. Would I find in your dossier the answer to this question: Why did the man who killed the boy in broad daylight, with people around on the street, dare to run the risk of later identification by one or more onlookers? Or to this one: How

to account for the log of the earrings—bought by Mrs.
Fromm on May eleventh, worn by another woman on May
nineteenth, and worn by Mrs. Fromm on May twenty-
second? Have you found any trace of the earrings beyond
that? Worn by anyone at any time?"

"No."

"So I have provided my own answers, but since I can't
expound them without naming my candidate, that will
have to wait. Meanwhile—"

He halted because the door to the hall was opening. It
swung halfway, enough for Fred Durkin to slip past the
edge and signal to me to come.

I arose, but Wolfe asked him, "What is it, Fred?"

"A message for Archie from Saul."

"Deliver it. We're sharing everything with Mr. Cramer."

"Yes, sir. Horan wants to speak with you. Now. Urgent."

"Does he know Mr. Cramer and Mr. Stebbins are here?"

"No, sir."

Wolfe went to Cramer. "This man Horan is a hyena,
and he irritates me. I should think you would prefer to
deal with him on your own premises—and also the other
two. Why don't you take them?"

Cramer regarded him. He took the cigar from his mouth,
held it half a minute, and put it back between his teeth.
"I would have thought," he said, not positively, "that I
have seen you work all the dodges there are, but this is
new. I'm damned if I get it. You had Horan and that
lawyer Maddox here, and you chased them. The same with
Paul Kuffner. Now Horan and the other two, there in your
front room, and you don't even want to see them, and still
you claim you're after the murderer. I know you too well
to ask you why, but by God I'd like to find out." He
swiveled his head around to Fred. "Bring Horan in here."

Fred, not moving, looked at Wolfe. Wolfe heaved a
sigh. "All right, Fred."

14 For a second I thought Dennis Horan was actually going to turn and scoot. He came wheeling in like a man with a purpose, stopped short when he saw we had company, forward marched four steps, recognized Cramer, and stopped short again. That was when I thought he was going to skedaddle.

"Oh," he said. "I don't want to butt in."

"Not at all," Cramer assured him. "Sit down. We were just talking about you. If you've got something to say, go right ahead. I've been told how you happen to be here."

Considering the atmosphere and circumstances, including the hard night he had been through, Horan did pretty well. He had to make a snap decision whether to make any change in his program because of the unexpected presence of the law, and apparently he managed it while he was placing a chair between Stebbins and Cramer and putting himself on it. Seated, he glanced from Cramer to Wolfe and back to Cramer.

"I'm glad you're here," he said.

"So am I," Cramer rumbled.

"Because," Horan went on, "you may feel that I owe you an apology, though I may not agree." The tenor was down a couple of notches. "You may think I should have told you about a talk I had Friday evening with Mrs. Fromm."

Cramer was giving him a hard eye. "You have told us about it."

"Yes, but not all of it. I had to make an extremely difficult decision, and I thought I made it right, but now I'm not so sure. Mrs. Fromm had told me something that might prove damaging to the Association for the Aid of Displaced Persons if it were made public. She was the president of the Association, and I was its counsel, and therefore what she told me was a privileged communication. Ordinarily, of course, it is improper for an attorney to divulge such a communication, but I had to decide

125

whether this was a case where the public interest prevails. I decided that the Association had a right to rely on my discretion."

"I think the record will show that you gave no indication that you were withholding anything."

"I suppose it will," Horan conceded. "Possibly I even stated I had told you all that was said that evening, but you know how that is." He thought he would smile and then thought he wouldn't. "I had made a decision, that's all, and now I think it was wrong. At least I now want to reverse it. After dinner that evening Mrs. Fromm took me aside and told me something that shocked me greatly. She said she had received information that someone connected with the Association was furnishing names of people illegally in this country to a blackmailer, or a blackmail ring, and that the people were being persecuted; that the blackmailer, or the head of the ring, had been a man named Matthew Birch, who had been murdered Tuesday night; that a man named Egan was involved in it; and that—"

"Aren't you Egan's attorney?" Cramer demanded.

"No. That was a mistake. I acted on impulse. I've thought it over, and I've told him I can't act for him. Mrs. Fromm also told me that the meeting place of the blackmailers was a garage on Tenth Avenue—she gave me its name and address. She wanted me to go there at midnight that night, Friday. She said there was a pushbutton on the second pillar to the left in the garage, and I should give a signal with it, two short, one long, and one short, and then go to the rear and down a stair to the basement. She left it to me how to proceed with whomever I might find there, but she impressed on me that the main thing was to prevent any scandal that would injure the Association. That was like her! Thinking always of others, never of herself."

He paused, evidently momentarily overcome. Cramer asked, "Did you go?"

"You know I didn't, Inspector. As my wife and I have told you, after I took Mrs. Fromm down to her car I returned to my apartment and went to bed. I had told Mrs. Fromm that I would think it over. I would probably have decided to go the next night, Saturday, but in the morning the news came of Mrs. Fromm's death, and that terrible shock—" Horan had to pause again.

He resumed. "Frankly, I was hoping that you would find the murderer, and that there would be no connection between the crime and the affairs of the Association. So I didn't tell you of that talk. But Sunday came and went, and Monday, and I began to fear that I had made a mistake. Last evening I decided to try something. Around midnight I drove to that garage, drove right in, and there on the second pillar found the pushbutton. I pressed it, giving the signal as Mrs. Fromm had told me, and an answering signal came, a buzzer. As I was starting for the rear a man who had been lurking nearby drew a gun and ordered me to go as he directed. I did so. He took me back to a stair and commanded me to descend. At the foot of the stairs was another man with a gun, whom I recognized—Archie Goodwin."

He nodded sidewise at me. I didn't return it. He went on. "I had seen him Saturday evening in this office. While I no longer feared for my own safety, naturally I resented having guns pointed at me, and I protested. Goodwin summoned another man from within a room, also armed, and I was taken across to a wall and held there. I had seen this other man previously. He had called at my office yesterday morning, giving the name of Leopold Heim, and I had—"

"I know," Cramer said curtly. "Finish the garage."

"As you wish, Inspector, of course. Before long Goodwin called to this man, calling him Saul, to bring me to the room. There were three other men in there, one obviously with Goodwin, and the other two lying on the floor with their ankles bound. Goodwin said he had telephoned Nero Wolfe, and apologized to me. Then, after he had spoken briefly to the two on the floor, saying they had committed felonies and he was going to take them to Wolfe for questioning, he told one of them, the one he called Egan, that I was a lawyer and I might be willing to represent him. When the man asked me I said I would, and I must confess that that was ill-considered. I explain it, though I don't ask you to excuse it, by the fact that I was not in proper command of my faculties. I had been ordered around by men with guns, and besides I resented Goodwin's arbitrary transport of those men to the house of his employer when the proper procedure would have been to notify the authorities. So I agreed, and came here with them, and have been held here all night. I—"

"No," I objected. "Correction. Not held. I told you several times you could go whenever you wanted to."

"*They were held*, and I was held by the foolish commitment I had made. I admit it was foolish, and I regret it. Considering these latest developments, I have reluctantly concluded that Mrs. Fromm's death may after all have had some connection with the affairs of the Association, or with one of its personnel, and in that case my duty is plain. I am now performing it, fully and frankly, and, I hope, helpfully."

He got out a handkerchief and wiped his brow, his face, and his neck all around. "I have had no chance for a morning toilet," he said apologetically. That was a damn lie. There was a well-equipped bathroom with doors both from the front room and the office, and he had been in it. If, not having then decided to be full and frank and helpful, he hadn't wanted to have Egan out of his sight long enough to wash his face, that was his affair.

Cramer's hard eye hadn't softened any. "We're always grateful for help, Mr. Horan," he said, not gratefully. "Even when it's a little late. Who heard your talk with Mrs. Fromm?"

"No one. As I said, she took me aside."

"Did you tell anyone about it?"

"No. She told me not to."

"Who did she suspect of being implicated?"

"I told you. Matthew Birch, and a man named Egan."

"No. I mean who connected with the Association."

"She didn't say. My impression was that she suspected no one in particular."

"From whom had she got her information?"

"I don't know. She didn't tell me."

"That's hard to believe." Cramer was holding himself in. "She had a lot of details—Birch's name, and Egan's, and the name and address of the garage, and even the button on the pillar and the signal. She didn't tell you where she got all that?"

"No."

"Did you ask her?"

"Certainly. She said she couldn't tell me because she had been told in confidence."

Our four pairs of eyes were on him. He kept his, with their swollen red lids and long curled lashes, at Cramer. All of us, including him, understood the situation perfectly. We knew he was a damn liar, and he knew we knew it. He had been in a hole up to his neck, and this was his try at scrambling out. He had had to cook up some explanation for his going to the garage, and especially for the push-button and his signaling with it, and on the whole it wasn't a bad job. Since Mrs. Fromm was dead he could quote her all he wanted to, and since Birch was dead too there was no risk in naming him. Egan had been his problem. He couldn't ignore him, since he was right there in the next room. He couldn't stick to him, since to act as attorney for a blackmailer whose racket was being exposed—and the exposure would hurt the Association, of which Horan was counsel—that was out of the question. So Egan had to be tossed to the wolves. That was it from where I sat; and, knowing the other three as well as I did, and seeing their faces as they looked at him, that was it from where they sat too.

Cramer turned to Wolfe with his brows raised in inquiry. Wolfe shook his head.

Cramer spoke. "Purley, bring Egan."

Purley got up and went. Horan adjusted himself in his chair, getting solider, and sat straight. This was going to be tough, but he had asked for it. "You realize," he told Cramer, "that this man is evidentially a low criminal and he is in a desperate situation. He is scarely a credible witness."

"Yeah," Cramer said and let it go at that. "Goodwin, how about a chair for him there near you, facing this way?"

I obliged. That would put Stebbins between Egan and Horan. Also it would give Wolfe Egan's profile, but since he offered no objection I placed the chair as requested. As I was doing so Stebbins returned with Egan. "Over here," I told him, and he steered Egan across. Sitting, the low criminal fastened his eyes on Dennis Horan, but they weren't met. Horan was watching Cramer.

"You're Lawrence Egan," Cramer said. "Known as Lips Egan?"

"That's me." It came out hoarse, and Egan cleared his throat.

"I'm a police inspector. This is Nero Wolfe. I'll soon have a report on you. Have you got a police record?"

Egan hesitated, then blurted, "The report will tell you, won't it?"

"Yes, but I'm asking you."

"Better go by the report. Maybe I've forgot."

Cramer passed it. "That man next to you, Archie Goodwin, has told me what happened yesterday, from the time you called on a man at a hotel on First Avenue—you thought his name was Leopold Heim—until you were brought here. I'll go over that with you later, but first I want to tell you where you stand. You may be thinking that you have an attorney present to protect your interests, but you haven't. Mr. Horan says he has told you that he can't represent you and doesn't intend to. Did he tell you that?"

"Yes."

"Don't mumble. Speak up. Did he tell you that?"

"Yes!"

"When?"

"About half an hour ago."

"Then you know you're not represented here. You're facing two charges, assault with a loaded gun and attempted extortion. On the first one there are two witnesses, Fred Durkin and Archie Goodwin, so that's all set. On the second one you may be thinking there's only one witness, Saul Panzer alias Leopold Heim, but you're wrong. We now have corroboration. Mr. Horan says that he was told last Friday evening, by a reliable person in a position to know, that you were involved in a blackmailing operation, extorting money from people who had entered the country illegally. He says that his agreement to represent you was given on an impulse which he now regrets. He says he wouldn't represent a low criminal like you. He—"

"That's not what I said!" Horan squeaked. "I merely—"

"Shut up!" Cramer barked. "One more interruption and out you go. Did you say you were told that Egan was in a blackmail racket? Yes or no!"

"Yes."

"Did you say you won't represent him?"

"Yes."

"Did you call him a low criminal?"

"Yes."

"Then shut up if you like it here." Cramer went to Egan. "I thought you had a right to know what Mr. Horan said, but we won't need that to make the extortion stick. Leopold Heim wasn't the first one, and don't think we can't find some of the others. That's not worrying me any. I want to ask you something in Mr. Horan's presence. Had you ever seen him before last night?"

Egan was chewing his tongue, or anyhow he was chewing something. Some saliva escaped at a corner of his mouth, and he wiped it away with the back of his hand. His jaws still working, he interlaced his fingers and locked them tight. He was having a hell of a time.

"Well?" Cramer demanded.

"I gotta think," Egan croaked.

"Think straight. Don't kid yourself. We've got you like that"—Cramer raised a fist—"on the assault and the extortion. It's a simple question: Had you ever seen Mr. Horan before last night?"

"Yeah. I guess so. Look, how about a deal?"

"No. No deal. If the DA and the judge want to show some appreciation for cooperation, that's up to them. They often do, you know that."

"Yeah, I know."

"Then answer the question."

Egan took a deep breath. "You're damn right I saw him before last night. Lots of times. Dozens of times." He leered at Horan. "Right, brother? You goddam lousy rat."

"It's a lie," Horan said calmly, meeting the leer. He turned to Cramer. "You invited this, Inspector. You led him into it."

"Then," Cramer retorted, "I'll lead him some more. What's Mr. Horan's first name?"

"Dennis."

"Where is his law office?"

"One-twenty-one East Forty-first Street."

"Where does he live?"

"Three-fifteen Gramercy Park."

"What kind of a car does he drive?"

"A fifty-one Chrysler sedan."

"What color?"

"Black."

"What's his office phone number?"

"Ridgway three, four-one-four-one."

"What's his home number?"

"Palace eight, six-three-oh-seven."

Cramer came to me. "Has this man had any chance to acquire all that information during the night?"

"He has not. No part of it."

"Then that will do for now. Mr. Horan, you are being detained as a material witness in a murder case. Purley, take him to the other room—who's in there?"

"Durkin and Panzer, with that Ervin."

"Tell them to hold Horan, and come back."

Horan stood up. He was calm and dignified. "I warn you, Inspector, this is a blunder you'll regret."

"We'll see, Mr. Horan. Take him, Purley."

The two left the room, Purley in the rear. Cramer got up and crossed to my wastebasket, dropped the remains of his cigar in it, and returned to the red leather chair. He started to say something to Wolfe, saw that he was leaning back with his eyes closed, and didn't say it. Instead he asked me if he could be heard in the next room, and I told him no, it was soundproofed. Purley came back and went to his chair.

Cramer addressed Egan. "Okay, let's have it. Is Horan in that racket?"

"I want a deal," Egan said stubbornly.

"For God's sake." Cramer was disgusted. "You're absolutely sewed up. If I had a pocketful of deals I wouldn't waste one on you. If you want a break, earn it, and earn it quick. Is Horan in the racket?"

"Yes."

"What's his tie-in?"

"He tells me how to handle things, like people that are trying to get from under. Hell, he's a lawyer. Sometimes he gives me leads. He gave me the lead on that Leopold Heim, goddam him."

"Do you deliever money to him?"

"No."

"Never?"

"No, he gets his cut from Birch. He did."

"How do you know that?"

"Birch told me."

"How did you get in it?"

"Birch. He propositioned me about two years ago, and I gave it a run. Three or four months later there was some trouble with a guy over in Brooklyn, and Birch fixed it for me to meet a lawyer at the garage to get a steer on it, and the lawyer was Horan. That was the first time I saw him. Since then I've seen him—I don't know, maybe twenty times."

"Always at the garage?"

"Yeah, always. I never met him anywhere but there, but I've talked with him on the phone."

"Have you got anything in Horan's handwriting? Anything he ever sent you or gave you?"

"No."

"Not a scrap? Nothing?"

"I said no. That cagey bastard?"

"Was anyone else present at any of your meetings with Horan?"

"Sure, lots of times Birch was there."

"He's dead. Anyone else?"

Egan had to think. "No."

"Never?"

"Not down in the basement with us, no. The night man at the garage, Bud Haskins, of course he saw him every time he came." Egan's eyes lit up. "Sure, Bud saw him!"

"No doubt." Cramer wasn't stirred. "Horan's ready for that, or thinks he is. He'll meet it by putting the word of a reputable member of the bar against the word of a low criminal like you backed up by a pal that he'll say you have primed. I'm not saying Haskins can't help. We'll get him, and we'll—where you going?"

Wolfe had pushed his chair back, got to his feet, and taken a step. He looked down at Cramer. "Upstairs. It's nine o'clock." He passed between his desk and Cramer and was on his way.

Cramer protested. "You actually—you walk out just when—"

"When what?" Wolfe demanded. Halfway to the door, he had turned. "You've got this wretch cornered, and you're clawing away at him for something to implicate another wretch, that unspeakable Horan, in the most contemptible enterprise on record. I admit it's necessary, indeed it is admirable, but I've contributed my share and you don't need me; and I'm not after blackmailers, I'm after a murderer. You know my schedule; I'll be available at eleven o'clock. I would appreciate it if you'll remove these miserable creatures from my premises. You can deal with them just as effectively elsewhere."

"You bet I can." Cramer was out of his chair. "I'm taking your men along, all four of them—Goodwin, Panzer, Durkin, and Cather—and I don't know when we'll be through with them."

"You make take the first three, but not Mr. Cather. He isn't here."

"I want him. Where is he?"

"You can't have him. He's on an errand. Haven't I given you enough for one morning? Archie, do you remember where Orrie has gone?"

"No, sir. Couldn't remember to save me."

"Good. Don't try." He turned and marched out.

15 I have never seen as much top brass in one day as I did during the next eight hours, from nine in the morning to five in the afternoon that Tuesday, one week from the day Pete Drossos had called to consult Wolfe about his case. At the Tenth Precinct station house it was Deputy Police Commissioner Neary. At 240 Centre Street it was the Commissioner himself, Skinner. At 155 Leonard Street it was District Attorney Bowen in person, flanked by three assistants, including Mandelbaum.

It didn't go to my head because I knew it wasn't just my fascinating personality. In the first place, the murder of Mrs. Damon Fromm, linked as it was with two other murders, was still, after four days, good for a thousand barrels of ink per day, not to mention the air waves. In the second place, the preliminary jockeying for a mayoralty election had started, and Bowen and Skinner and Neary were all cleaning fish ready for the fry. A really tiptop murder offers some fine possibilities to a guy who is so devoted to public service that he is willing to take on additional burdens in a wider field.

At Manhattan Homicide West, at the Tenth Precinct, we were separated, but that was okay. The only items we were saving were the crisscross we had used on Egan and his notebook, and Saul and Fred knew all about that. I spent an hour in a little room with a stenographer, getting my statement typed and read and signed, and then was taken to Cramer's office for a session with Deputy Commissioner Neary. Neither Cramer nor Stebbins was there. Neary was gruff but chummy. His attitude implied that if they would just leave him and me alone for forty minutes we'd have it all wrapped up, but the trouble was that in less than half that time he got a phone call and had to let me go. As I was escorted along the corridor and downstairs and out to where a car was waiting, city employees I barely knew by sight, and others I didn't know from Adam, made a point of greeting me. Apparently the impression was around that I was going to get my picture in the paper, and who could tell, I might get drafted to run for mayor. I acknowledged the greetings as one who appreciated the spirit in which they were offered but was awful busy.

At Leonard Street, Bowen himself, the District Attorney, had a copy of my statement on his desk, and during our talk he kept stopping me, referring to the statement, finding the place he wanted and frowning at it, and then nodding at me as if to say, "Yep, maybe you're not lying after all." He didn't congratulate me on collaring Ervin and Egan and tricking Horan in. On the contrary, he hinted that my taking them to Wolfe's house instead of inviting cops to the garage was probably good for five years in the coop if only he had time to read up on it. Knowing him as I did, I overlooked it and tried not to upset him. The poor guy had enough to contend with that day without me. His weekend had certainly been bollixed up, his eyes were red from lack of sleep, his phone kept ringing, his assistants kept coming and going, and a morning paper had put him fourth on the list of favored candidates for mayor. Added to all that, the FBI would now be horning in on the Fromm-Birch-Drossos case, on account of the racket Saul and Fred and I had removed the lid from, with the painful possibility that the FBI might crack the murders. So it was no wonder the DA didn't ask me out to lunch.

In fact nobody did. It didn't seem to occur to anyone that I ever ate. I had had an early breakfast. By the time the session in Bowen's room broke up, a little after twelve, I had in mind a place around the corner I knew of that specialized in pigs' knuckles and sauerkraut, but Mandelbaum said he wanted to ask me something and took me down the hall to his room. He got behind his desk and invited me to sit, and started in.

"About that offer you made yesterday to Miss Estey."

"My God. Again?"

"It looks different now. My colleague Roy Bonino is up at Wolfe's place now, inquiring about it. Let's cut the comedy and go on the basis that Wolfe sent you to make her that offer. You say yourself that there was nothing improper about it, so why not?"

I was hungry. "Okay, if that's the basis, then what?"

"Then the presumption is that Wolfe knew about this blackmail racket before he sent you to make that offer. He was assuming that Miss Estey would be vitally interested in knowing whether Mrs. Fromm had told Wolfe about it. I don't expect you to admit that; we'll see what Wolfe tells Bonino. But I want to know what Miss Estey's reaction was—exactly what she said."

I shook my head. "It would give you a wrong impression if I discussed it on that basis. Let me suggest a basis."

"Go ahead."

"Let's say that Mr. Wolfe knew nothing about any racket but merely wanted to stir them up. Say he didn't single out Miss Estey, she was just first on the list. Say I made the offer not only to her, but also to Mrs. Horan, Angela Wright, and Vincent Lipscomb, and would have gone on if Mr. Wolfe hadn't called me in because Paul Kuffner was at the office accusing me of putting the bee on Miss Wright. Wouldn't that be a more interesting basis?"

"It certainly would. Uh-huh. I see. In that case I want to know what they all said. Start with Miss Estey."

"I'd have to invent it."

"Sure, you're good at that. Go ahead."

So there went the best part of another hour. When I was all through inventing, including answers to a lot of bright questions, Mandelbaum got up to leave and asked me to wait there. I said I would go get something to eat, but he said no, he wanted me on hand. I agreed to wait, and there went another twenty minutes. When he finally returned he said Bowen wanted to see me again, and would I kindly go to his room. He, Mandelbaum, had something else on.

When I got to Bowen's room there was no one there. More waiting. I had been sitting awhile, thinking of pigs' knuckles, when the door opened to admit a young man with a tray, and I thought hooray, someone in this joint is human after all; but without even glancing at me he went to Bowen's desk, put the tray down on the desk blotter, and departed. When the door had closed behind him I stepped to the desk and lifted the napkin, and saw and smelled an attractive hot corned-beef sandwich and a slab of cherry pie. There was also a pint bottle of milk. The situation required presence of mind, and I had it. It took me maybe eighteen seconds to get back to my chair, settle the tray in my lap, and bite off a healthy segment from the sandwich. It was barely ready for swallowing when the door opened and the District Attorney entered.

To save him any embarrassment, I spoke up immediately. "It was darned thoughtful of you to have this sent in, Mr. Bowen. Not that I was hungry, but you know the old saying, we must keep the body up with the boy. Bowen for mayor!"

He showed the stuff he was made of. A lesser man would either have grabbed the tray from me or gone to his desk and phoned that a punk had swiped his lunch and he wanted another one, but he merely gave me a dirty look and turned and went. In three minutes he was back with another tray, which he took to his desk. I don't know whose he confiscated.

What he wanted was to clear up eighty-five or ninety points about the report Mandelbaum had just given him. So it was nearly three o'clock when I arrived, escorted, at

240 Centre Street, and going on four when I was ushered
into the private office of Police Commissioner Skinner. The
next hour was a little choppy. You might have thought
that, with a citizen as important as me to talk with, Skinner
would have passed the order that he wasn't to be disturbed
for anything less than a riot, but no. Between interruptions
he did manage to ask me a few vital questions, such as was
it raining when I got to the garage, and had any glances of
recognition been exchanged by Horan and Egan, but
mostly, when he wasn't answering out of the four phones
on his desk, or making a call himself, or speaking with some
intruder, or taking a look at papers just brought in, he was
pacing up and down the room, which is spacious, high-
ceilinged, and handsomely furnished.

Around five, District Attorney Bowen walked in, accom-
panied by two underlings with bulging briefcases. Apparently there was to be a high-level conference. That might
be educational, if I didn't get bounced, so I unobtrusively
left my chair near Skinner's desk and went to a modest one
over by the wall. Skinner was too occupied to notice me,
and the others evidently thought he was saving me for
dessert. They gathered chairs around the big desk and went
to it. I have a good natural memory, and it has been well
trained in the years I have been with Nero Wolfe, so I
could give a full and accurate report of what I heard in the
next half-hour, but I'm not going to. If I did I would go
sailing out the next time I tried being a wallflower at a
meeting of the big brains, and anyway who am I to destroy
the confidence of the people in their highly placed public
servants?

But something did happen that must be reported. They
were in the middle of a hot discussion of what should and
what should not be told to the FBI when an interruption
came. First a phone rang and Skinner spoke into it briefly,
and then a door opened to admit a visitor. It was Inspector
Cramer. As he strode across to the desk he darted a glance
at me, but his mind was on higher things. He confronted
them and blurted, "That man Witmer that thought he
could identify the driver of the car that killed the Drossos
boy. He just picked Horan out of a line. He thinks he'd
swear to it."

They stared at him. Bowen muttered, "I'll be damned."

"Well?" Skinner demanded crossly.

Cramer frowned down at him. "I don't know, I just this minute got it. If we take it, it twists us around again. It couldn't have been Horan in the car with the woman Tuesday. We couldn't budge his Tuesday alibi with a bulldozer, and anyway we're assuming it was Birch. Then why did Horan kill the boy? Now that we've got that racket glued to him, of course we can work on him, but if he's got murder on his mind we'll never crack him. We've got to take this and dig at it, but it balls it up worse than ever. I tell you, Commissioner, there ought to be a law against eyewitnesses."

Skinner stayed cross. "I think that's overstating it, Inspector. Eyewitnesses are often extremely helpful. This may prove to be the break we've all been hoping for. Sit down and we'll discuss it."

As Cramer was pulling up a chair a phone rang. Skinner got it—the red one, first on the left—talked to it a little, and then looked up at Cramer.

"Nero Wolfe for you. He says it's important."

"I'll take it outside."

"No, take it here. He sounds smug."

Cramer circled around the desk to Skinner's elbow and got it, "Wolfe? Cramer speaking. What do you want?"

From there on it was mostly listening at his end. The others sat and watched his face, and so did I. When I saw its red slowly deepening, and his eyes getting narrower and narrower, I wanted to bounce out of my chair and beat it straight for Thirty-fifth Street, but thought it unwise to call attention to myself. I sat it out. When he finally hung up he stood with his jaw clamped and his nose twitching.

"That fat sonofabitch," he said. He backed off a step. "He's smug all right. He says he's ready to earn the money Mrs. Fromm paid him. He wants Sergeant Stebbins and me. He wants the six people chiefly involved. He wants Goodwin and Panzer and Durkin. He wants three or four policewomen, not in uniform, between thirty-five and forty years old. He wants Goodwin immediately. He wants Egan. That's all he wants."

Cramer glared around at them. "He says we'll be bringing the murderer away with us. The murderer, he says."

"He's a maniac," Bowen said bitterly.

"How in the name of God?" Skinner demanded.

"It's insufferable," Bowen said. "Get him down here."

"He won't come."

"Bring him!"

"Not without a warrant."

"I'll get one!"

"He wouldn't open his mouth. He'd get bail. Then he'd go home and do his own inviting, not including us."

They looked at one another, and each saw on the others' faces what I was seeing. There was no alternative.

I left my chair, called to them cheerily, "See you later, gentlemen!" and walked out.

16 I have never been on intimate terms with a policewoman but have seen a few here and there, and I must say that whoever picked the three to attend Wolfe's party that afternoon had a good eye. Not that they were knockouts, but I would have been perfectly willing to take any one of the trio to the corner drugstore and buy her a Coke. The only thing was their professional eyes, but you couldn't hold that against them, because they were on duty in the presence of an inspector and so naturally had to look alert, competent, and tough. They were all dressed like people, and one of them wore a blue number with fine white stripes that was quite neat.

I had got there enough in advance of the mob to give Wolfe a brief report of my day, which didn't seem to interest him much, and to help Fritz and Orrie collect chairs and arrange them. When the first arrivals rang the bell Orrie disappeared into the front room and shut the door. Having been in there for chairs, I had seen what he was safeguarding—a middle-aged round-shouldered guy wearing glasses, with his belt buckled too tight. Orrie had introduced us, so I knew his name was Bernard Levine, but that was all.

The seating arrangement had been dictated by Wolfe.

The six females were in a row in front, with the police-women alternating with Angela Wright, Claire Horan, and Jean Estey. Inspector Cramer was in the red leather chair, with Purley Stebbins at his left, next to Jean Estey. Back of Jean Estey was Lips Egan, within reach of Stebbins in case he got nervous and started using pliers on someone, and to Egan's left, in the second row, were Horan, Lipscomb, and Kuffner. Saul Panzer and Fred Durkin were in the rear.

I said Cramer was in the red leather chair, but actually it was being saved for him. He had insisted on speaking privately with Wolfe, and they were in the dining room. I don't know what it was he wanted, but I doubted if he got it, judging from the expression on his face as he marched into the office ahead of Wolfe. His jaw was set, his lips were tight, and his color was red. He stood, facing the gathering, until Wolfe had passed to his chair and got into it, and then he spoke.

"I want it understood," he said, "that this is official only up to a point. You were brought here by the Police Department with the approval of the District Attorney, and that makes it official, but now Nero Wolfe will proceed on his own responsibility, and he has no authority to insist on answers to any questions he may ask. You all understand that?"

There were murmurs. Cramer said, "Go ahead, Wolfe," and sat down.

Wolfe's eyes moved left to right and back again. "This is a little awkward," he said conversationally. "I've seen only two of you before, Mr. Horan and Mr. Kuffner. Mr. Goodwin has provided me with a chart, but I'd like to check. You're Miss Jean Estey?"

"Yes."

"Miss Angela Wright?"

She nodded.

"Mrs. Dennis Horan?"

"That's my name. I don't think—"

"Please, Mrs. Horan." He was brusque. "Later, if you must. You're Mr. Vincent Lipscomb?"

"Right."

Wolfe's eyes went back and forth again. "Thank you. I believe this is the first time I have ever undertaken to single out a murderer from a group mostly strangers. It seems a

little presumptuous, but let's see. Mr. Cramer told you I
have no authority to insist on answers to questions, but I'll
relieve your minds on that score. I have no questions to ask.
Not one. As I go along an occasion for one may arise, but I
doubt it."

Cramer let out a low growl. Eyes went to him, but he
didn't know it. He was fastened on Wolfe.

"I shall indeed ask questions," Wolfe said, "but of myself, and answer them. This affair is so complex that they
could run into the hundreds, but I'll constrain myself to
the minimum. For instance, I know why Mrs. Fromm
wore those golden spiders on her ears when she came to see
me Friday noon, they were a part of her attempted imposture; but why did she wear them Friday evening to the
dinner party at Horan's? Obviously in the hope of surpris-
ing a reaction from someone. Again for instance, why did
Mr. Horan go to the garage last night? Because he knew his
greed had impelled him to a foolish action, giving Leopold
Heim's name and address to Egan at this juncture, and he
was alarmed—as it turned out, with reason. I suppose—"

"I protest!" Horan's tenor was squeaking. "That's slander! Inspector Cramer, you say Wolfe speaks on his own
responsibility, but you're responsible for getting us here!"

"You can sue him," Cramer snapped.

"Mr. Horan." Wolfe aimed a finger at him. "If I were
you I'd stop lathering about your implication in blackmail.
On that you're sunk, and you know it, and now you're
confronted with a much greater danger, identification as
the murderer of Peter Drossos. You can't possibly escape a
term in jail, but with my help you may go on living. When
we finish here you're going to owe me something."

"You're damned right I am!"

"Good. Don't try to pay it, either in your sense or in
mine. I was about to say, I suppose most of you know nothing about the extortion enterprise that has resulted in the
death of three people, so you can't follow me throughout,
but that can wait. One of you will assuredly be able to
follow me."

He leaned forward a little, with his elbows on the chair
arms and his ten fingertips resting on the desk. "Now. I
don't pretend that I can do the pointing unaided, but I
have had intimations. The other day one of you was at

pains to tell Mr. Goodwin of your movements Friday evening and Tuesday afternoon, though there was no earthly reason why you should have bothered. The same one made a strange remark, that it had been fifty-nine hours since Mrs. Fromm had been killed—extraordinary exactitude! Those were worth filing as intimations, but no more."

He clasped his hands in front of his middle mound. "However, there were two major indications. First, the earrings. Mrs. Fromm bought them on May eleventh. Another woman was wearing them on May nineteenth. She must have got them as a gift or loan from Mrs. Fromm, or obtained them surreptitiously. In any case, Mrs. Fromm had them back and wore them three days later, Friday the twenty-second—and why? To try to impersonate the woman who had been wearing them on Tuesday! Then she knew who that woman was, she had some kind of suspicion about her, and, most important as an indication, she was able to retrieve the earrings, either openly or by stealth, for the purpose of the impersonation."

"Indication of what?" Cramer demanded.

"Of the woman's identity. By no means conclusive, but suggestive. She must have been one whose person and belongings were easily accessible, whether Mrs. Fromm retrieved the earrings overtly or covertly. Certainly that was in your calculations, Mr. Cramer, and you explored it to the utmost, but without result. Your formidable accumulation of negatives in this affair has been invaluable to me. Your ability to add two and two is unquestioned. You knew that my newspaper advertisement about a woman wearing spider earrings appeared Friday morning, and that Mrs. Fromm came here Friday noon wearing them, and that it was a good working hypothesis that she had retrieved them in that brief interval—two or three hours at the most. If she had had to go afar to get them you would have discovered it and exploited the discovery, and you wouldn't be here now. Isn't that true?"

"You're telling it," Cramer growled. "I didn't know they were bought by Mrs. Fromm until this morning."

"Even so, you knew they were probably unique. By the way, an interesting speculation as to why Mrs. Fromm bought them when they caught her eye in a window. Mr. Egan has said that in phoning to him a woman used a password, 'Said a spider to a fly.' Possibly, even probably, Mrs. Fromm had overheard that peculiar password used, and indeed that may have been a factor in her suspicion; and when she saw the spider earrings the impulse struck her to play a game with them."

Wolfe took in a chestful of air, with him at least a peck, and let it out audibly. "To get on. The man who ran the car over the boy, Pete Drossos, was a strange creature, hard to swallow and impossible to digest. The simplest theory, that he was the man who had been in the car with the woman the day before, and was afraid that the boy could and would identify him, was invalidated when I learned that the man in the car with the woman had been Matthew Birch, who was killed Tuesday night; but in any case his conduct was peculiar. I put myself in his place. For whatever reason, I decide to kill that boy by driving to that corner in broad daylight, and, if and when he appears and offers an opportunity, run the car over him. I can't expect the rare luck of having the opportunty at my first try; certainly I can't count on it; I must anticipate the necessity of driving through that intersection several times, perhaps many times. There will be people around. There will be no reason for any of them to note me particularly until my opportunity comes and I run over the boy, but I will be casually seen by many eyes."

He turned a palm up. "So what do I do? I can't wear a mask, of course, but there are other expedients. A false beard would be excellent. I scorn them all and make no effort to disguise myself. Wearing my brown suit and felt hat, I proceed with the hazardous and mortal adventure. Then manifestly I am either a peerless dunce, or I am a woman. I prefer it that I'm a woman, at least as a trial hypothesis.

"For if I'm a woman many of the complexities disappear, since most of the roles are mine. I am involved in the blackmailing project; it may be that I direct it. Mrs. Fromm gets wind of it—not enough to act on, but enough to make her suspicious. She asks me guarded questions. She gives me the spider earrings. Tuesday afternoon I meet Matthew Birch, one of my accomplices. He has me drive his car, which is unusual, and suddenly produces a gun and presses its muzzle against me. Whatever the cause of his hostility,

I know his character and I fear for my life. He orders me to drive somewhere. At a corner where we stop for a red light a boy approaches to wipe my window, and to his face, there so close to me, I say with my lips, 'Help, get a cop.' The light changes, Birch prods me, and we go. I recover from my panic, for I too have a character. Wherever we go, somewhere, sometime, I catch him off guard and attack. My weapon is a hammer, a wrench, a club, his own gun—but I don't shoot him. I have him in the car, helpless, unconscious, and late at night I drive to a secluded alley, dump him out, run the car over him, park the car somewhere, and go home."

Cramer rasped, "I could do this well myself. Show something."

"I intend to. The next day I decide that the boy is a threat not to be tolerated. If Mrs. Fromm should somehow verify her suspicions and my connection with Birch is exposed, the boy could identify me as Birch's companion in the car. I bitterly regret my moment of weakness when I told him to get a cop, startling him into staring at us, and I cannot endure the threat. So that afternoon, dressed as a man, I get the car from where it was parked and proceed as already described. This time I park the car far uptown and take the subway home.

"By now of course I am a moral idiot, an egomaniacal sow with boar's tusks. Friday morning Mrs. Fromm gets the spider earrings and leaves the house wearing them. When she came home late that afternoon she talked with me, and told me among other things that she had hired Nero Wolfe to investigate. That was very imprudent; she should at least have suspected how dangerous I was. That night she got proof of it, though she never knew it. I went and found her car parked not far from the Horan apartment and hid behind the front seat, armed with a tire wrench. Horan came down with her, but—"

"Hold it!" Cramer snapped. "You're charging Jean Estey with murder, with no evidence. I said you're responsible for what you say, but I got them here, and there's a limit. Give me a fact, or you're through."

Wolfe made a face. "I have only one fact, Mr. Cramer, and that hasn't been established."

"Let's hear it."

"Very well, Archie, get them."

As I got up to go to the connecting door to the front room I saw Purley Stebbins pay Wolfe one of the biggest tributes he ever got. He turned his head and dropped his eyes to Jean Estey's hands. All Wolfe had done was make a speech. As Cramer had said, he hadn't produced a sliver of evidence. And Jean Estey's face showed no sign of funk. But Purley, next to her, fastened his eyes on her hands.

I pulled the door open and called, "Okay, Orrie!"

Some heads turned and some didn't as they entered. Orrie stayed in the rear, and I conducted Levine through the crowd to a chair that was waiting for him at the corner of my desk, from which he had an unobstructed view of the front row. He was trying not to show how nervous he was, but when he sat he barely got onto the edge of the chair, and I had to tell him to get more comfortable.

Wolfe addressed him. "Your name is Bernard Levine?"

"Yes, sir." He licked his lips.

"This gentleman near the end of my desk is Inspector Cramer of the New York Police Department. He is here on duty, but as an observer. My questions are my own, and you answer at your discretion. Is that clear?"

"Yes, sir."

"My name is Nero Wolfe. Have you ever seen me before this moment?"

"No, sir. Of course I've heard of you—"

"What is your business, Mr. Levine?"

"I'm a partner in B. and S. Levine. My brother and I have a men's clothing store at Five-fourteen Fillmore Street in Newark."

"Why are you here? How did it happen? Just tell us."

"Why, there was a phone call at the store, and a man said—"

"Please. When?"

"This afternoon about four o'clock. He said his wife had bought a felt hat and a brown suit at our store last week, last Wednesday, and did we remember about it. I said sure I remembered, I waited on her. Then he said so there wouldn't be any mistake would I describe her, and I did. Then he—"

"Please. Did he describe his wife or ask you to describe the customer?"

"Like I said. He didn't do any describing. He asked me to, and I did."

"Go ahead."

"Then he said he wanted to come and maybe exchange the hat and would I be there and I said yes. In about half an hour, maybe a little more, in he came. He showed me a New York detective license with his picture on it and his name, Orvald Cather, and he said it wasn't his wife that bought the suit, he was investigating something. He said he was working for Nero Wolfe, the great detective, and something had come up about the suit and hat, and he wanted me to come to New York with him. Well, that was a problem. My brother and I don't like any trouble. We're no Brooks Brothers, but we try to run a nice honest little business—"

"Yes. But you decided to come?"

"My brother and I decided. We decide everything together."

"Did Mr. Cather give you any inducement? Did he offer to pay you?"

"No, he just talked us into it. He's a good talker, that man. He'd make a good salesman. So we came together on the tube, and he brought me here."

"Do you know what for?"

"No, he didn't say exactly. He just said it was something very important about the suit and hat."

"He didn't give you any hint that you were going to be asked to identify the woman who bought the suit and hat?"

"No, sir."

"He hasn't shown you any photographs, any kind of pictures, of anyone?"

"No, sir."

"Or described anyone?"

"No, sir."

"Then you should have an open mind, Mr. Levine. I'm asking you about the woman who bought a brown suit and a felt hat at your store last Wednesday. Is there anyone in this room who resembles her?"

"Sure, I saw her as soon as I sat down. The woman there on the end." He pointed at Jean Estey. "That's her."

"Are you positive?"

"One hundred per cent."

Wolfe's head swiveled. "Will that do for a fact, Mr. Cramer?"

Of course Jean Estey, sitting there between the sergeant and the policewoman, had had four or five minutes to chew on it. The instant she saw Levine she knew she was cooked on buying the outfit, since S. Levine would certainly corroborate B. Levine. So she was ready, and she didn't wait for Cramer to answer Wolfe's question, but answered it herself.

"All right," she said, "it's a fact. I was an utter fool. I bought the suit and hat for Claire Horan. She asked me to, and I did it. I took the package—"

The seating arrangement worked out fine, with the policewomen sandwiched among the civilian females. When Mrs. Horan shot out of her chair to go for Jean Estey, she got stopped so promptly and rudely that she was tossed clear to the lap of the policewoman on the other side, who made an expert catch. In the row behind them some of the males were on their feet, and several voices were raised, among them Inspector Cramer's. Purley Stebbins, now naturally a little confused, left Jean Estey to his female colleague and concentrated on Dennis Horan, who was out of his chair to rescue his wife from the clutches of the lady official who had caught her on the fly. Horan, feeling Purley's heavy hand on his shoulder, jerked away, drew himself up, and spoke to whom it might concern.

"That's a lie," he squeaked. He pointed a shaking finger at Jean Estey. "She's a liar and a murderer." He turned to direct the finger at Lips Egan. "You know it, Egan. You know Birch found out she was hogging it, she was giving him the short end, and you know what Birch meant when he said he would handle her. He was a damn fool to think he could. Now she's trying to hang a murder on me, and she'll suck you in too. Are you going to take it?"

"I am not," Egan croaked. "I've been sucked in enough. She can fry, the crazy bitch."

Horan turned. "You've got me, Wolfe, damn you. I

know when I'm through. My wife knew nothing about this, absolutely nothing, and I knew nothing about the murders. I may have suspected, but I didn't know. Now you can have all I do know."

"I don't want it," Wolfe said grimly. "I'm through too. Mr. Cramer? Will you get these vermin out of my house?" He turned to the assemblage and changed his tone. "That applies, ladies and gentlemen, only to those who have earned it."

I was opening the bottom drawer of my desk to get out a camera; Lon Cohen of the Gazette had earned, I thought, a good shot of Bernard Levine sitting in Nero Wolfe's office.

17 At eleven in the morning three days later, a Friday, I was at my desk typing a letter to an orchid collector when Wolfe came down from the plant rooms and entered. But instead of proceeding to his desk he went to the safe, opened it, and took something out. I swiveled to look because I don't like to have him monkeying with things. What he took was Lips Egan's notebook. He closed the safe door and started out.

I got up to follow, but he turned on me. "No, Archie. I don't want to make you accessory to a felony—or is it a misdemeanor?"

"Nuts. I'd love to share a cell with you."

He went to the kitchen, got the big roasting pan from the cupboard, put it on the table, and lined it neatly with aluminum foil. I sat on a stool and watched. He opened the looseleaf notebook, removed a sheet, crumpled it, and dropped it into the pan. When a dozen or more sheets were in the pile he applied a match, and then went on adding fuel to the flame, sheet after sheet, until the book was empty.

"There," he said in a satisfied tone, and went to the sink

to wash his hands. I tossed the book cover in the trash basket.

I thought at the time he was rushing things a little, since it was still possible they would need some extra evidence. But that was many weeks ago, and now that Horan and Egan had been duly tried, convicted, and sentenced, and it took a jury of seven men and five women only four hours to hang the big one on Jean Estey—what the hell.

ABOUT THE AUTHOR

REX STOUT, the creator of Nero Wolfe, was born in Noblesville, Indiana, in 1886, the sixth of nine children of John and Lucetta Todhunter Stout, both Quakers. Shortly after his birth, the family moved to Wakarusa, Kansas. He was educated in a country school, but, by the age of nine, was recognized throughout the state as a prodigy in arithmetic. Mr. Stout briefly attended the University of Kansas, but left to enlist in the Navy, and spent the next two years as a warrant officer on board President Theodore Roosevelt's yacht. When he left the Navy in 1908, Rex Stout began to write freelance articles, worked as a sightseeing guide and as an itinerant bookkeeper. Later he devised and implemented a school banking system which was installed in four hundred cities and towns throughout the country. In 1927 Mr. Stout retired from the world of finance and, with the proceeds of his banking scheme, left for Paris to write serious fiction. He wrote three novels that received favorable reviews before turning to detective fiction. His first Nero Wolfe novel, *Fer-de-Lance*, appeared in 1934. It was followed by many others, among them, *Too Many Cooks, The Silent Speaker, If Death Ever Slept, The Doorbell Rang* and *Please Pass the Guilt*, which established Nero Wolfe as a leading character on a par with Erle Stanley Gardner's famous protagonist, Perry Mason. During World War II, Rex Stout waged a personal campaign against Nazism as chairman of the War Writers' Board, master of ceremonies of the radio program "Speaking of Liberty" and as a member of several national committees. After the war, he turned his attention to mobilizing public opinion against the wartime use of thermonuclear devices, was an active leader in the Authors' Guild and resumed writing his Nero Wolfe novels. All together, his Nero Wolfe novels have been translated into twenty-two languages and have sold more than forty-five million copies. Rex Stout died in 1975 at the age of eighty-eight. A month before his death, he published his forty-sixth Nero Wolfe novel, *A Family Affair*.